Dreams of Poison. Copyright © 2014 by Solange nicole. MoonBeam Publishing.

First Edition: 2014

Cover Illustration and Book Design © 2014 Nikki Skie
Cover Photo: @ Stock

Reference Credit
Macbeth. Shakespeare, William. 1623
Pride & Prejudice. Austen, Jane. 1813

ISBN: 0985907584
ISBN: 978-0-9859075-8-7

Printed in the United States of America.

Dreams of Poison

Final Book in the Beloved Series

A
Novel

Un roman

SOLANGE NICOLE

Moonbeam Publishing
Houston, Texas

Dedicated to those who saw me through.
- And to those who didn't.

And then i saw him again
Every cell in my body
Awakened
And i decided then
i could no longer stay
Dormant

i cannot hide.

-K.G. O'Connell

PROLOGUE

Her heart raced as she turned the corner. The sound of her heels clattered against the pavement, echoing to the beat of her pulse. She hoped she could reach them in time. If not, it would be too late. Everything she worked for would vanish. She picked up the pace as she neared another corner in her crisp suit. Aimless fidgeting proved a useful tool as she waited for the pedestrian sign. The frantic attempt to fight her nerves. As she turned the corner, the stark white brick confronted her. Her stilettos quickened, fretting over the oncoming interview.

As much as Helen wanted to resent her mother, she couldn't help but thank her. The outfit she was wearing wasn't the only thing Ms. Vivian Rose afforded her in the past year. Helen was promptly chauffeured around the Upper East Side after she graduated with honors. Her mother introduced her at parties and opened doors she couldn't have on her own. The pang of déjà vu flooded Helen as she was once again paraded around in voyeuristic solidarity.

Yesterday, her mother had insisted she attend the year's biggest charity ball. Helen didn't want to go, but with no excuse of school she went. It *was* a change from her usual haunts of the Ward and their Touraine residence. Her mother had sold her Riverside home to be closer to her daughter. She couldn't go back to Glenwood. Helen refused to remember anything that happened during the second half of junior year and the beginning of senior—

The following semester was shrouded in black and fog. So many days bled into each other, Helen just let it all go. The sweet dankness of incoherency won out to the pain of clarity. Vivian was far from amused, reuniting with her inebriated daughter. Why she didn't have her committed sight-on-scene she'll never know. Maybe it was redemption for her vanity.

This mother, Vivian Rose, never had a fondness for weakness. Not even in herself. Despite what Helen believed, she did love her. Why else would she have given up her passion for art and become a psychiatrist? Although Vivian was good with people, she didn't enjoy the company of sociopaths and aging schizophrenics. Over the years the late hours and patient interventions took their toll. The painter, who wanted to open La Rose Studio, closed in on herself. The vivacious gleam died from her eyes. The only thing that kept her going was her little girl.

Vivian tried to be there for Helen. She brought her out to see a ballet when she had missed her recital. But, Helen's mother knew that not being present for her first performance could not be smoothed over with Swan Lake and sorbet. It was the only ballet she had ever seen. And, it would be the only recital her mother would ever hear about.

For the more Vivian tried to make up for her mistakes, the more Helen had begun to resent her for it. And, eventually push her away altogether. The divorcée had let her career come before her family. It was what blinded her from seeing any of the signs. There was no room in her plans for a neglected daughter and an untouched husband. After the papers were signed, she buried herself further into her patients' lives; and zealously forgot her own. Helen paid the price ever since her ninth birthday.

In her mind, finding Helen that day was godsend. *This* time would make up for all the rest. Vivian chose to surprise her daughter with some Earl Grey and a potted plant of morning glories on her 25th birthday. She rode the elevator up, pleased as punch with her little plan.

As she reached her daughter's apartment, Vivian happily knocked. Her eyes shifted to the door next to her. A man had emerged from an impossible darkness. She peered closer at him, taking in his ridiculously pale pallor and unusual pair of eyes. When he happened to turn and look at her, their eyes locked. He averted his eyes as if in shame. Vivian puzzled at what had the young man so out of sorts. She couldn't help but watch him awkwardly shuffle away. She roused herself when he disappeared around the corner to the elevator.

I wonder if he knows my daughter. The thought of her baby girl entertaining a man with such awkward comportment made her scoff. The idea was ludicrous. She turned back and knocked louder. Cocking her ear she anticipated footsteps that refused to sound. Apprehension seized Vivian as she searched her bag for the spare. She had insisted that Helen give her one since she was the primary leaser. Wasting no time, Mother Rose made her way into the living room.

"Helen?" She peeked into the bathroom and turned the lights off. Backtracking, Ms. Rose placed the flowers and tea on the counter. Eyeing the cardboard clutter and piles of clothing, she picked herself a pathway to the desk. She sighed and put everything on the couch. In front of her was a bottle of some very cheap wine. It might as well have come in a box. Vivian picked it up in disgust to inspect. Moving on, she placed it back down and spotted her daughter. Helen was sprawled out on the floor.

She gasped and rushed over to her daughter. One look at the grotesque red stain and Vivian's cell was dialing

911. As the dispatcher asked about the situation, she patted the stain and brought her fingers to her nose. A repulsed sound escaped her pursed lips as she stood from the floor.

"Do forgive my urgency, *false alarm*. It would seem my daughter is face down in a bottle of wine. Thank you but there will be no need for your services." She snapped the cell closed and nudged her child in her side. Helen groaned into the carpet.

Vivian sighed. "Well I *was* here to wish you a happy birthday. I see now you've already kicked off the festivities by your lonesome." She stood over Helen with her hands on her hips.

"Get up!"

"What the hell do you want from my life?" Helen bubbled out. Slowly, she turned her face out of the garnet puddle and toward her warden. The look on her mother's face was saying *right now*. The daughter snorted in response. That face used to scare her as a child. Now, it was just sad.

"Look at you! You need help! Come on." She bent down and hefted her grown child to a sitting position. She let go of Helen's arms only to watch them drop back to the ruddy carpet. Vivian's nostrils twitched as the trapped odor escaped from Helen and rose into the air. Instinctively, she stepped back and grabbed her nose.

"I'm beyond help." Helen bitterly muttered. She struggled to get off the floor only to blunder her way to the couch.

"What is wrong with you? And what is that smell!"

Helen winced at the raised pitch in the woman's voice. She raised her hand as if to block the noises from happening, "Shhh you're loud," she softly scolds.

"Helen Marie Lane, are you out of your senses? What is the meaning—" Vivian looked about the room before finishing "—of all this mess? I did not pay thousands of dollars for you to do *this* to your home. To my investment."

Helen chortled darkly at her mother's financial concerns. *God forbid she ever actually be worried about me*, Helen mused.

"Glad you think this is funny. You are coming with me young lady and you are checking into rehab!" Vivian grabbed for her arm. Helen sobered up and blocked her mother's hand.

"Vivian-" Helen yelled out, her mother winced at her own name. Her daughter ignored the grimace. "I'm not going to rehab," she finished softly.

"Well you must do something." She beseeched her college graduate. "Come on, let's get you cleaned up and go out for your birthday. Girls' night out!"

Helen sighed and rolled her eyes when her mother turned away. Reluctantly, she got up and followed after to the bathroom. Her eyes roll bigger as Vivian turned the corner.

Her mother echoed out, "And you must do something with that hair!"

Part One
Chapter One

Carmen languidly scratches his hair; an arm thrown back behind his head. His jungle physique languid on the leather seat. He yawns at the victim screaming on the floor. Evey's goon kicks the American once more for effect.

"D'accord- enough." Bored, he rouses himself and swings his legs out in front of him. Carmen crouches down before the kneeling American. A lazy smile shadows as he leers forward.

"Did you think that Mme. Evelyn would not find out about the $50,000 you owe her? Hmm?" He plucks him in the forehead and grabs him by the chin. The thick Occidental accent dripping with each word.

The pitiful drug dealer whimpers as Carmen releases him. He watches as the Frenchman wipes his hand, disgusted, on a handkerchief. Looking from the discarded napkin to his captor, the American silently beseeches. Seeing no change in the psychopath, he moves to speak. A hand strikes drawing blood and a weak groan from its blow. The goon retracts his arm, satisfied the *cafard* wouldn't open his mouth again.

Angry tears burn down as that blond bitch's pup turns towards him. The pitiful sounds betray him when Carmen resumes his perch. Looking him over, the

American resents just how young this guy is. He blisters as the sick bastard grins again. Why couldn't they just kill him already? Why the torture? Was waterboarding *next*?

Smelling the suited man's fear, Carmen grins. "*Now that I've got your attention*, this is what you're going to do. You're going to persuade your business associate to go into this deal with us. That way Mme. gets her funding and Monsieur Voyou lets you keep *tes rotules*."

Risking the impending pain, "What's that?" He winces, bracing himself. In its wake, laughter rivets. Confused, he looks up to see the two criminals snickering. Carmen stands and levels him with a balmy gaze.

"Your kneecaps." He purrs. Smirking one last time, he turns to Voyou and pats him on the chest. The gruff man snorts in return and bends down to bring the suit to his feet. He snarls until the man cowers. Voyou jeers yanking him out into the alley and into an idling car.

———

Carmen sighs and plops back into his chair. His fingernails catch his attention. Pulsating lights strain through the frosted glass and skip across the bloody nail beds. He looks up to a pair of tits standing in front of his face. Disgusted, he continues on up to mascaraed eyelashes and puckered red lips.

"Mon chér, really, nail biting is a nasty habit." Evey muses affectionately. Carmen stares at her blankly. Pulling his finger away he spits the sanguine juice out onto the black speckled floor. Evey watches as it arcs and lands a few feet away from her. The smirk tightens beneath the crinkling of her eyes.

Not willing to break so easy, he resumes with a fresh nail. He chooses the hangnail on his third finger. Evey sniffs, indignant, as she walks over to her desk in the far corner.

"How was work?" She draws out sweetly.

Carmen launches bloody spittle, hangnail and all in hasty reply.

The tolerant smile freezes as her patience wanes. She swings her spiked heels out from under the desk. In one swift motion she confronts him allowing her waistline to be center view. Carmen feigns a look, catching the hint of aggravation. The apathetic chuckling threatens to break her resolve.

Unwavering, she leans forward meeting his eyes evenly. "My dove, I understand you are upset about your dirty fingernails." Her eye twitches noting his lack of submission. "But that does not give you the right to spit all over my office!"

She halts waiting for his rebuttal. Her sanity suffers as he reluctantly gazes up at her. All desire to maim ceases as her breath hitches. Knowing he has her, his gaze intensifies burning its way into her dark heart. Thoughts of work slip through the hour glass of her mind as she weakens. She could never get anything done with him around. *C'est impossible.* The very reason Evelyn conducted business outside of the club. Or wherever *he* wasn't.

In a tumultuous rush, their bodies collide against the desk. Carmen impatiently growls as he swipes the contents onto the floor. Evey giggles as he slams her against the surface. Moans escape as they ravage each other.

———————

Disgust rolls in as the fog of post coitus recedes. He scoffs as he looks down at her limp body. Stuffing his blouse back into his slacks, Carmen wastes no time readying to leave. He shivers off the last of the shame as he melts into the crowd. A noxious drug he couldn't help but take once more. Only to regret it once the high was over. He felt ravenous for her, but couldn't stand the sight of her, when Helen's jaded green eyes blazed within him.

Helen. She haunted him those first few months after that disastrous run in at the Kaffe. He couldn't find any reprieve from the pain. Every dark haired beauty was her. Green eyes made him wince near the corner café or across the street.

The very last time he was at Glenwood, a strange older woman had caught his attention. Dr. Rose. He had only seen her in pictures but he recognized her all the same.

He recalled the memory as their eyes met. A year before, he had found old photos beneath Helen's bed. She was out in the kitchen making breakfast when he decided to stretch out on the edge. To pass the time, his fingers made their way down his sides and under the skirts. Reaching around his hand landed soundly on a box. He pulled it out next to his feet and flipped the lid. His eyes lit up at a childhood photo of his Goddess. Carmen melted at the sight of six year old Helen in full riding gear beside a beautiful horse.

Sifting through the box, his deft fingers found an austere portrait of a woman. She posed severely with her dark hair falling just so on her shoulders. Carmen canted his head at the woman's expression, wondering if this was her mother. He never got to ask. Hearing her rustling down the hall Carmen dropped the photo back into the box. He soundly pressed the cover down and slid it back into place. He bolted upright in surprise when Helen made her way through the door with a tray full of food.

"What were you doing?" She stopped, puzzled.

His eyes regained their glossy composure as he went into a mock stretch. "Stretching." He grinned hoping to throw her off. Her mouth quirked into a confused smile. She shook her head and sat down on his lap, feeding him a fresh strawberry.

Carmen shook the memory off and scuttled past Dr. Vivian Rose outside Helen's door. He hadn't dared go back since. How could he after what he'd done? After what he was doing now? Living with the guilt of choosing Evey, in the end. Dying every day knowing Helen could never know he did it for her.

But he couldn't think about that anymore. Not now. Not when he was clearly scrotum-deep with Evey. Nothing short of death would pry her grip off of him. He was her plaything once again and there was no way around that. At her beck and call, he had to do whatever she wanted, whenever she wanted. *And then some.*

Carmen had toyed around with the idea of giving into her completely. What was the point of trying to hold onto something he could never get back? He had sunk into a chasm since Helen walked out, and hadn't the strength to crawl back out. A year after that horrible day, consumption of bloodlust, money, and blow had begun to swirl around his mind as the nostalgic toxins had set in.

Instead of fighting out of habit, Carmen let it poison his broken heart. Letting it swill around the wounds and slosh his senses until he saw red. It didn't take long before he felt right at home among the filth. Nights were spent ordering up drinks and harassing the customers at Pulse. That is until Evelyn jerked him in line and gave him busy work. Now, he laundered people for money and had the occasional run in with murder.

But no matter what he did, Helen was there to haunt him. She was there when he turned out the light. She was there when he looked in the mirror. She was there every time he was with Evey. *Those eyes.* Those chillingly soulful, jaded, green eyes. He knew now his punishment wasn't a lifetime with Evelyn—but endless days and nights with those eyes.

Chapter Two

Helen was finding it hard to resist the routine she had fallen into since she had started assisting at Avenues. Such a wonderful school; and the children were so smart and engaging, she couldn't help but fall in love with them. It had only been a couple of months since that intimidating interview. She had to remember to take her mother out to dinner some time to thank her properly. These new surroundings of the Empire State, the Hudson, and the High Line were enough to keep her spirits up any day.

Walking through the glass doors, Helen makes her way past the parent café. The sounds of orchestra and toddlers banging on drums emanate from the main music center. She reaches the main stairs and makes her way to the fourth floor: the Lower School. She greets all the children and they all welcome her in unison. She beams at them as she sits down beside their teacher. Helen sighs contentedly as she pulls out her notebook and begins her observation.

—

When she returns to The Touraine later that day, she lets her mind drift. Shadows held captive by the sun, slither closer nipping at her heels. Begging her to join them. Clutching the familiar place around her waist, she hunches her way to the library. Defeated by the effort to hold herself together, Helen slumps in the grand chair before the fire place. The haunted chimes of the grandfather clock mark the dismal dissent into oblivion.

Numbly, she tucks her feet underneath and grabs the afghan from behind. She burrows deep within her father's old chair and sighs. Her eyes glaze over staring into the fire one of the maids had prepared. They had become so accustomed to her strange habits, Helen had want for very little.

One breezes by the room to check in. She tip toes close enough to ask Miss Helen what she needed. A once over and she shakes her head, leaving as she'd come. Helen barely registers the woman's presence.

Alone, Helen's mind slips into the familiar darkness. Flashes of Evey poison her mind as she remembers everything she's lost. The once seizing grip that the pain had had on her heart was cooled now to a dull ache. She still couldn't think of—she snaps her gaze up and away from the fire. The inky blackness swirls above her head threatening to overtake her at any moment. She breathes deeply struggling to push against it.

Clutching at what used to be her heart, she doubles over losing the evening battle. Then and *only* then, did she let his face penetrate her mind. *Carmen.* Bitter sweet pain ripples through her as she rides out the momentary relapse. His smoky eyes and bewitching lips steal her breath. The way he would hold her. Those few fleeting moments of bliss. His lips shaped her name so perfectly it made her weak in the knees.

Helen grips her hair in torment as the memories play out on the silver screen behind her lids. Carmen, sweet, vulnerable, sexy *Carmen.* Carmen, the man she thought she could trust. The one she would have loved forever. Carmen the man who broke her heart and left her for dead. Left her for that poisonous bitch.

It was clear to her now, Happiness was a seductive illusion. No one as fucked up as her deserved one drop of joy. But oh god was it delicious when it fell into her lap for a little while. *Such a pretty face*, she bitterly muses, *with such a bruised and battered soul.* When the dawn of a promise fades into the dusk of reality, all that remains is the nightmare. Sweet, sweet loneliness. Shadows come to play and prey on her beaten mind. Her lovely little dreams of poison.

As the depression drains to a dull murmur, she leans back. A deep sigh relieves her tight chest. She turns to the vanity table next to her. Her face falls as she sees a Riedel full of pinot noir. Someone must've placed it there while she was… distracted. A hard gulp stops halfway down her throat as she eyes the blood red temptation. Twelve months of renewed sobriety would wash away with just one sinful taste. Tentatively she reaches out for it, her hand shaking. Fearful of someone watching, her eyes shift to the hallway and she recoils. When no one appears, she resumes her trance. *Just a tiny sip.* One sip to appreciate the bouquet placed in front her. Her tongue absently licks from side to side as her fingers twitch towards the stem. Giddily, she snatches the glass closer and stares into the sanguine bliss. For one moment there's peace. The familiar ecstasy of anticipation snakes around and seeps within her. Just. One. Taste.

Her heavy breathing halts as she throws the glass back and downs the wine in seconds. She moans relishing the rich dry taste as it rolls around her tongue. She licks her lips and leans back in the chair. When the pleasure fades her eyes open in alarm. She looks down at the empty glass and cries out. Clasping her mouth she slams it back down on the tray. Her face falls into her hands as the guilt consumes her. She sobs at the realization that it wasn't even enough to blot out the remorse setting in. Abruptly, she sits up—her crying cuts off as she hears an unmistakable clink. She faces the butler horror stricken. In his hand was a carafe of ruby liquid. He pours more into the glass without a word. Their eyes meet briefly. Her childhood friend quirks a smile and vanishes. Leaving her no time to protest.

Helen blinks through her daze. Didn't they know she had a drinking problem? She looks down to see the carafe glinting against the fire light. Well if they did, they certainly didn't show it. *Or object.* Taking a deep breath she reaches for the second glass.

Chapter Three

Carmen couldn't wait to get his hands on a blade. The sudden urge to carve and peel someone's flesh takes a hold of him. Blood *was* always better than sex for him anyway. It just so happened, in this arrangement, one ensued the other. Especially when it was Evey he was fucking. Instead of a cigg, he wanted to torture something. Or someone.

He thinks of the pathetic American from earlier and his lips twitch. The veneer of a sneering grin and chilling gaze grace the customers of Pulse as he makes his way out of the door.

Sliding his hand along the damp brick wall, he slinks out into the night. He snaps up when he hears a sound. Spotting the rat he scoffs to himself. Picking up the pace, he makes his way out of the alley and onto the street. He puts his hands in his pockets and straightens as he joins rush hour. Walking amongst the crowd gives him time to think. It usually helped him to forget what he had just done moments before.

The idea of fileting someone was tempting though. A woman catches his eye as she walks by. He leers at her and she grimaces. Carmen chuckles to himself imagining the creeped out thoughts she must be having. He looks up laughing to himself and falters. Across the street he sees *her*. His heart hammers in his chest and he tries to swallow back the panic. Quickly, he ducks through the crowd to get closer.

Helen was walking past the café. *Their* café. She pointedly ignores it and clutches her books closer to her chest. Carmen sighs drinking in her beauty. God! he missed her! And it always hurt when he was reminded of just how much. He hesitates and blends into the crowd when her head turns his way. Did she see him? He hopes for her sake, she didn't.

Anger coils through him as he watches the imaginary Manhattan scene fade from view... What was he thinking, pining over her like that? He shakes his head and pushes his way forward trying to shake the hallucination. He needed to inflict pain. Now.

Carmen pulls out his cell and taps on his contacts. With the Suit's address on screen, he back tracks and turns around. Rounding the corner, Carmen heads back to the club for a car. This was going to take a while.

———

He parks down the street on Valley Road. He scoffs as he looks around the neighborhood. Despite what he thought of the American, he wasn't surprised he lived in Montclair, New Jersey. *Helen would've loved a house like this.* He stops the thought in its tracks. Carmen stalks up the pathway leading to the front door. Hearing laughter inside, he sneaks off the path to the nearest window. Peering inside, he sees the American and his family.

A quaint scene of a wholesome family sitting around in the living room playing a board game. The rage pitters out of his body as he huffs. He couldn't kill a man with a family like this. Carmen gazes at the picturesque scene for a little longer. It wasn't too long ago he wanted his own version of this. A life now barred from him.

Helen... He closes his eyes and sees her breathtaking smile. Absently, his hand makes its way into his jean pocket. His fingers loop around the ring inside. He twists it around like he's done so many times before. His eyes open and see Helen and their children sitting around the coffee table. Carmen, sitting at the head shaking the dice, a playful smile on his lips. Helen leans over and sneaks a kiss when the kids prattle on about which property they're going to buy next.

His eyes shut tight squeezing out the tears that had been building. He lets go of the ring in his pocket and rubs his eyes. When his vision clears he turns back down the path and heads for the car. His face blisters as the toll of what he's lost caves in on him once again. His knuckles whiten as he grips the wheel putting the Jag in drive. *Fuck this.* He peels out and turns out of the suburban neighborhood.

The American whips his head up and peers out the window. His wife turns to him distraught and clasps his hand. He relaxes as the comforting silence follows the alarming screech. At least for now, he'll live to see another day with his family.

———

Carmen parks the car near the back entrance of Pulse. He stalks out into the alleyway hunched in his leather jacket. His hand that had played with the engagement ring, twiddles now with a spring assist. He walks out onto the dark street and heads out to anywhere Evelyn isn't. Scanning the street, Carmen searches for someone to sate him. Moving further down the block, he reaches the unlit sidewalk. The grin slowly reappears as he spots a group of thugs walking towards him.

His icy gaze trains on a straying member. The stumbling drunken thug slurs his goodbyes. Carmen slithers in his direction in the shadows. He follows as the boy struggles to walk. He turns back to see the teen's friends head further down the opposite direction. Carmen sneers and creeps forward.

He flinches as the inebriated criminal bursts into an obscure hip hop song. He shakes his head at the most likely suburban Caucasian runaway struggling to make his way past a dumpster. The blood lust rises and makes him shiver. Carmen stalks closer, his steps conspicuously splashing through the alley. The boy turns and shouts a friendly insult. His face falls not recognizing Carmen. He hollers at the stranger to stay back. Clumsily, he pulls out a blade and raises it in the air.

His stalker leers at him as he moves closer to him. Carmen lets the adrenaline swim through his veins as he gains on the little thug. He drinks in the familiar wide eyed look and rolls his head from side to side. He laughs under his breath as the boy tries to take off. Carmen breaks into a breathless sprint after him. He stops as the frightened teen reaches a wire fence.

Carmen chuckles darkly at the kid's drunken stupidity. *Too easy.* He slows coming up on the boy scrambling to climb. Clucking disapprovingly, he shakes his head. The thug looks down at him.

"What the fuck do you want from me man?"

Carmen chuckles and raises his hands up at the fence. "Surely, you should've known this was here." A menacing grin slips.

"So, I took a wrong turn! Screw you man I don't need this shit. Just leave me alone okay?" The shaken criminal looks down at Carmen desperately wishing for him to disappear.

He shakes his head at the boy and clucks. His accent snakes unctuously around the teen's ears. "No. No I think I won't". He laughs when his face pales in response. Stepping closer he grabs a hold of the chain and rattles him. Laughter echoes off the wet brick as he antagonizes the boy further. Frightened completely, the thug frantically kicks at Carmen's hands and face.

He laughs with each blow. Each resounding kick sends the Marseillan's senses reeling. A delicious tingle shoots down his spine as his head snaps from side to side. He shivers devouring the pain. When the boy tires, he pants taking stock of the damage he has done. His eyes widened in panic watching the creep spit blood and chuckle darkly. Slow to move, Carmen carefully turns his head forward and then up at the dangling ruffian. A bloody grin on a foot printed face greets him.

"*My turn.*"

Carmen yanks the boy down the fence. He shivers as he screams out for help. *Yes, that's it. Scream for me.* Carmen yanks with purpose a second time sending the boy hurtling to the ground. With a wet smack the boy groans unable to move. Lunging for him, the deranged Frenchman drags him to his feet. Seething in his face, he looks the kid over. Moving to his ear, Carmen's breath slows and his voice lowers.

"*Run.*"

The teen lifts his eyes to see if this guy is serious. Not taking any chances, he slams his hands down over Carmen's and takes off. He stumbles through the gutters and tries to run out of the alley. Picking himself up and raising his pants he scrambles out of the alley.

Carmen grins watching the drunken idiot run for his life. The jungle cat springs into action and gains on him. The boy turns to see that he's following and tries to run faster. Instead of losing him he spurs his attacker on. Carmen rushes up behind him, catching his arm. Wrenching it behind him Carmen overtakes the criminal and drives his knife deep in his side.

The climatic gasps swirl around Carmen as he cradles the thug to the ground. Turning him onto his back he gazes into the boy's murderous glare. He smiles and tenderly caresses his cheek. He coos at him.

"Don't worry... This *will* hurt, but not for long."

The thug sobers at the whispered declaration and tries to fight Carmen off. His head cracks against the asphalt as Carmen raises him and slams him back down.

"Now that I have got your attention," he lilts.

He brings his blade into view and lets it glint off the lone street lamp. Satisfied by the boy's horrified gaze he slowly skims the knife along his skin. He clamps a hand down around his mouth as he expertly skins the middle of his forehead. The muffled screams fade into the background as Carmen's vision bloodies.

Images of Helen staring at him in muted disgust. Evey's sweaty body rolling beneath him. The dark lust rising in him every time Evelyn comes near. Helen's heartbreaking dash out of the coffee shop disappearing forever. Carmen thrusting inside of Evey clasping her throat and slamming her back down onto the desk. The blood of their first victims smearing against their sweaty bodies as they laugh and writhe. Carmen diving between Evey's thighs and digging his nails into her flesh. Helen's innocent sighing as he worships her beneath the moonlit sky. The resounding slaps that make Carmen's eyes roll in the back of his head when he takes Evey from behind. Helen's soft feathery caresses down his chest when he thrusts deep inside her. The swift gripping tug of his hair as his head is jerked backwards in Evelyn's grasp. Helen's green eyes lost and alone. He and Evelyn laughing as they tortured and killed. Their lips crushing against each other violently to the sounds of screaming. Carmen swooning beneath Evey's ensnaring embrace.

Surfacing from the haze, Carmen glares wildly at the bloodied corpse. His knife had peeled and skinned perfectly the young man's face. Slowly, he lifts his hand off of the still warm muscle tissue. His fingers were covered in the blood he had slathered in. His other hand dripped with blood from both blade and skin. He stares blankly at his *mains sanglantes*. The comforting wet feeling of their caressing embrace soothes Carmen. His head tilts from side to side as he revels in the smearing of his face. He coos and moans and licks both palms as they make their way over his mouth. He halts their motion and drives them through his hair and sighs.

Looking up into the starless sky, he relaxes. His shoulders slump and he hums contentedly as his face stains with the drying blood. After a few deep breaths, he looks back down at the faceless criminal. He cants his head and peels his eyes at his handiwork. He gazes at the boy for a few moments, pensive. A solemn mood darkens over Carmen.

"I'm getting sloppy." He exclaims. He runs a hand through his hair and looks at the nearby dumpster. Grabbing hold of the corpse he drags it to a standing position, and hoists it over his shoulder. After dumping the body, he retraces and picks the flesh up off the pavement. He grabs a stray newspaper and wraps the pile. Chunking it in with the body, Carmen lowers the lid, and nods. Out of habit he wipes his hands together, as if to rid himself of the dumpster and corpse's coodies.

Shoulders relaxed, Carmen wipes his knife clean, pockets it and heads back down the street. He lazily surveys the empty streets as he nears the back entrance to Pulse. When reaching the door, he pats Voyou's back and smiles as he passes him on the way in. Dutifully ignoring the man's confused questioning gaze. Carmen casually jogs up the stairs leading back up to the office. A satisfied smile resting on his lips. He makes himself at home as he languidly splays back out on the couch.

"There you are mon chér." Evey greets him after just settling in. Carmen looks over at her, masking his startled disgust. "Go clean up. When I get back from this errand, we'll resume our earlier *meeting.*" Evey giggles and winks at Carmen as she walks out the door. He flinches weakly.

Chapter Four

Helen lets the crystal slip from her fingers and onto the chair. Doubled over, her eyes glaze as they lose themselves in the fire. The carafe was empty now, but she didn't care. The damage is done. She absently wipes her mouth dry. With great effort, she lifts back against the cushion of her father's great chair. Her head rolls to the side. She chuckles at the night air completely detached. Now to relax and let her mind unwind. The wine will keep her from wincing at the memories.

She still couldn't believe how stupid she'd been. Sleeping with a guy she'd just met after stalking her all the way home. Falling in love only a few months into the relationship. Then, meeting his ex. That blond bitch. How could she have thought everything would be okay? Helen scoffs at her feline jealousy of the woman. She was a fool to think she could compete with *that*.

Helen's mind slips to that moment again when she found Chad and Evey. Knowing what she does now she should've killed that slut. She chuckles huskily at the idea of pointing a .45 at them. Pulling the trigger right as Evey opens her mouth. Finally putting it to good use.

She caves beneath the darkness and the blood spills across her mind. Evelyn's blood. *His* blood. Her…blood. Helen gasps ignoring the suicidal rush of ecstasy. *No*, she rebukes. *I'd want to make them pay, first.* She imagines she couldn't really pull the trigger or plunge the knife. But that didn't stop her from having fun picturing it. What she wouldn't give to have some of those moments back.

Helen would've waited until after she found the two of them in the café. Waited until they had left and headed back to Evey's to reunite *properly*. She would've followed and kept to the shadows. There was two ways Helen would've taken revenge. The first plays out before her. She'd have waited until they reached her place and got into bed. Standing quietly behind the cracked door, she'd have watched them. Let the scene of Carmen fucking Evey fuel her rage and give her courage. With each thrust she would blink back the tears and steel her resolve. And just as they were about to climax, Helen would open the door completely and slowly cock the revolver. And as the cold metal clicking caught their attention she'd smile. Soaking in their shocked expressions and horrified gazes she'd move closer to the bed. Patiently goading them to beg for forgiveness. Just as Carmen raises his hand to speak her name, she'd pull the trigger. After that bullet seared through his brain and Evelyn's screams filled her ears, she'd cock it again and silence the room forever.

The daydream puts a vicious smile on Helen's lips. *But*, there's always the more dramatic *beatific* way. Her patience would go beyond that horrendous confrontation and after graduation. She'd graduate with high honors and ambitiously search for internships. Reconnect with her mother and pretend to be happy with where her life was leading. The day Carmen decided to bring that whore to Glenwood, she would unearth the knife he gave her. The one from her 23rd birthday. Grab the key he made her as well. He never had the balls to ask for it back. Silently, she would make her way through the cashmere halls again.

Following the sounds of the grand canopy thudding against their shared wall. The wet slap of flesh pounding into each other perfuming her ears. Calmly she would stand in the doorway, unabashedly staring. Just to be polite Helen would allow them to writhe into a climax. Slowly, she'd make her way to the bedside as they panted in a sweaty heap. She'd have stood there quietly waiting out their afterglow. The knife making its way out of her pocket. To make it perfect, she'd move to the foot of the bed in full view. "I'm glad you're happy." She would hold his gaze as he looked up. Without breaking his gaze, Helen would raise the blade. Very gingerly, the knife would travel across her jugular. Unnervingly staring Carmen down. She would take those last seconds of life and climb into bed with them. Fall just so that she landed between them looking up at Carmen. Her undaunting green eyes and flowing red blood haunting him forever.

Helen rouses herself at last. She looks over to the side table. The carafe remains empty. She frowns, disappointed.

"Abbot, please do bring me another bottle. Make it red please." she shouts into the empty night hall. She sits expectantly. When the butler appears she smiles at him.

"What do you have for me?" she beams.

"My dear, I'm afraid—to give this to you." He reveals the bottle from behind his back. He holds it close warily looking her over.

"I need it more than *she* does." Helen scowls. Abbot's face darkens.

"And what am I to tell your mother? That her daughter is a drunk?" He raises a paternal brow. Helen drops her gaze sluggishly. Her mother could be easily ignored and scoffed at. Not Abbot, her only friend. The father she never had.

He softens with a sigh. Reluctantly, he places the bottle down. "Last one, do you hear me?" His warm voice reproaches. Helen looks at him as if a child granted conditional mercy.

"Yes, Abbot." Her eyes drop, chastened. Her butler relaxes and smiles.

"Goodnight, Miss Helen." He nods still smiling. Then, he's gone.

"Goodnight," she looks out into the shadows, "father." A hug from him right now is all she needed to forget about the alcohol and Carmen. Her mother put an end to those when she reached puberty. The bottle would have to do.

The minutes slosh by as her eyes swim deeper. Her cheek pressed to the hardwood floor, her hands palm out. Helen lies prostrate in front of the fire. A puddle of drool begins to form as her mind drips into unconsciousness.

Slowly, she comes to, a blinding light begging her hand to shield her eyes. Confusion and fear take over when she realizes she can't move her arm. Doing her best to adjust, the sounds of people talking and monitors beeping come into focus. Helen looks over to her arms to see bandages covering them. Frightened, she thrashes demanding someone to tell her what happened. Abbot comes closer to her and grabs her hand. His crisp uniform was rumpled, the sleeves rolled up and bloody.

"What is going on?" she pouts.

"It's ok, little dove. You're safe now." He tenderly strokes back her matted hair. His eyes red and swollen from crying.

"Why am I in the—hospital?" Helen looks about herself taking in the monitors, the IV, and the type AB blood bag holstered.

"You lost a lot of blood, Helen." Abbot gulps back the fresh tears and fails to smile.

"What?!" Helen panics raising the sound of the heart monitor. A nurse appears and checks the screen and in hushed tones advises Abbot to let her rest. Helen clings to her friend and shakes her head at the woman. "No, he stays." Reluctantly, the nurse leaves her side gifting the butler a weary gaze. Helen turns to him and begs him to tell her about the bandages. A hand flies to his mouth as he stifles back more tears. Rubbing his face he collects himself and looks Helen in the eye.

"Some time after we talked, some of the maids said you were passed out in front of the fire. When they came to check on you again, you were gone. They went looking for you. Bernita found you in your mother's room.

"She said you had gotten a hold of your father's old razors. The ones made of silver that your mother kept locked in her armoire.

"—You had cut yourself," Abbot pauses covering his mouth holding back a sob. "You were bleeding all over your mother's carpet. Bernita caught you slumped against her bed. She guessed you had smeared blood against your mother's white bedding. There were red streaks above and around your head." He pauses and drops his head again trying to find the strength to look his little dove in the eye.

"Thank God, she had discovered where you were in time. Any later and you could've—" Abbot loses control and sobs. Defeated, he slumps next to Helen. Helen weakly tries to comfort him. Then, she remembers her arms were strapped to the bed. Suicide watch, it makes sense to her now.

"Can you tell the nurse or whoever that I'm okay now? That I won't do it again?" Hopeful she looks into his bleary eyes. He sobs harder and looks away.

"You're under suicide watch for the next two days."

"Oh, I see." She softly replies.

Abbot turns to her, grabs her by the shoulders. "Promise me! Promise me you won't do another thing like this! I can't have you carrying on trying to kill yourself while you get piss drunk." Helen starts beneath his grip her eyes widening with each shouted exclamation.

A nurse comes running hearing the shouting from out in the hall. "Sir, you need to go. Please." Her stern gaze burns a hole into the back of Abbot. Begrudgingly, he lets go of Helen. His hands flapping to his sides. He drops his head and breathes deeply. "Sir—" the nurse urges him. Helen catches her attention and shakes her head and waves her hand. The nurse glares at her. She smiles back sheepishly. "Ten more minutes, and then he has to go."

"I'm sorry little bird. I'm sorry." Abbot shakes his head in grief not daring to look at her. Helen's eyes tear seeing the man who was always her strength fall further to pieces. She needed him to be strong now. More so than ever.

"Abbot—" Slowly, he sputters and raises his head. His shoulders slump and heave with each labored breath. Helen tries to smile. Weakly he mimics.

"I don't think I can do this on my own. I don't want to do this again. You're right, and it was stupid. I'll work through this and get better. Ok? Will you help me?"

Abbot manages to smile through his tears. Breathing deep he tries to collect himself once more. Clasping her hand he tenderly strokes her. "Of course, little dove." Helen beams hopeful at the man she called her father.

"You haven't called me by my pet names since I was a child."

"You will always be my little bird." He tickles her nose. Helen scrunches up and chuckles. They both laugh together. He sighs staring at the clock. "I guess I better go. I will be here first thing tomorrow." He nods sternly. His gaze warning her to behave until then. Helen shrinks beneath the paternal glare.

"Okay, Abbot." She softly yields. She smiles when he pats her hand and closes her eyes when he kisses her forehead. Her smile fades as she watches him walk out the door.

Helen jumps and snaps her gaze from the hallway at the nurse's voice.

"Your father is a sweet man. Most dads would go ballistic on their daughters for pulling a stunt like this." She double checks Helen's chart and inspects the IV. Helen warms and smiles shyly.

"Yes he is. And yes, I know." She settles back in her pillow as the nurse finishes up her routine check. *Your father* she replays it in her mind. *My father,* she softly muses. And with a beaming smile she drifts into a peaceful sleep.

———

"Helen!"

"Abbot!"

Helen beams as he walks through the door. Her eyes light up at his smile and the bouquet in his hand. Noticing her gaze he moves closer. He hands her the sunflowers and sits down next to her.

"I know they're not morning glories, your favorite, but these always remind me of you. And I thought since you're being discharged today—" he fiddles with a petal and smiles at her.

"I love them thank you." She pulls him in for a hug.

"I'm glad you like them. A dark woman named Zuey was selling them at a little stand. She told me to tell you that they bring good luck. I hope she's right." His eyes crinkle with the beaming smile. Helen can't help but beam back.

"I hope so too."

"Come on. Let's get you home." He gently helps her out of the bed and onto her feet. Helen shivers at the cold floor. Abbot reaches and hands her the change of clothes. She smiles and takes them to the bathroom. Fully changed and ready to go, Helen grabs her flowers and heads for the door. Her dutiful butler following behind.

In the elevator, they stand in companionable silence. Occasionally smiling at each other. The doors swing open and they make room for a couple with a newborn. Abbot shoots a look at Helen. She smiles at the happy tired couple. He relaxes as she makes small talk about the baby. A slow and dangerous bloom of hope fills him as he watches Helen try to change.

Abbot opens the passenger door and helps Helen in. He drives cautiously back to The Touraine. Sparing a glance here and there to make sure she's okay. He can't tell anything with her looking out the window.

Helen stares out at the road and passing buildings. She prays Vivian will go easy on her when she gets home from work. She better make some changes fast or she will for sure be seeing more of her mother. In a strait jacket. Abbot wouldn't let that happen though. He would protect her. Cautious, caring Abbot. She chuckles at his driving. Both hands on the wheel, *ten and four*. Nothing at all like the way Car—she stops the thought. She fakes a smile as she erases the rest of it. *That person no longer affects my life.*

She needs to prove to Abbot, her mother, and most of all herself, that she will survive this. It was time to spit out the poison she had been sucking on for the better part of the year. But she knows, in order to do that, she must think about them one last time. Taking a deep breath, she closes her eyes. She lets Carmen's face appear for the last time. Fighting back the ache and choked tears, she speaks to him. *I forgive you... Carmen.* She watches his hurt face fade to black. Helen straightens back her shoulders. The next person wasn't going to be easy.

Trying not to set her jaw on edge, she wipes away an escaping tear. Slowly, she makes peace with Evelyn. The sneering face enters her mind daring her to speak. Helen hesitates frightened. Calming herself, she musters the courage to look Evey in the eye. Evey arches a brow with a bemused smile. *I...* She falters and takes a few deep breaths. Helen stops to think about the love Abbot has for her, and the strength she's pulling from it. She lets the warmth rise within her. She looks back at Evelyn full of the peaceful warmth. *I forgive you.* She smiles at the confused vixen's face. *I do. I forgive you, Evelyn.* Helen beams when Evey loses all mirth and gazes at her. With a farewell nod, Evey fades from view.

She sighs into her seat as she lets the daylight and radio come back into focus. Helen looks over at her butler who was staring at her puzzling. She looks out the windshield. They were parked and in the garage. Cautiously, she beams at him. Still confused he smiles tentatively back.

"You were crying." He looks her over waiting for a break down. Something.

"I was." Helen wipes away the small tears. She smiles back at him. There was no needing to convince him it was real. She didn't need to fake it anymore.

"Shall we go up?"

"Is she home?"

"No." They smile at each other mischievously and make their way up to the apartment.

Once inside, they make their way to putting the sunflowers in a vase, and putting their belongings away. Abbot finds Helen in her room and grins.

"Shall I have Gloria make your favorite? We haven't used the wok in a while. Or shall I call for some take out?" He waves the house phone teasingly. Helen giggles and nods in agreement. "Good." He turns on his heels and heads back down the hall. "Get cleaned up we'll make an event of it. I shall find us a good film!"

Helen giggles again as she moves to the bathroom to freshen up. Her shower ends and she makes her way back to her room in a towel. She quirks an eyebrow when her cell rings. Drying her fingers she picks it up and answers.

"Hello—" She listens and frowns. After they've finished speaking, she hangs up. Helen chews her lip.

"Shit." Scurrying she reaches in her closet and pulls an ensemble together. She runs down the hall and grabs her shoes. Abbot catches her on the way out.

"What's wrong?"

Helen refuses to slow and as she heads out the door she yells back, "Rain check until tonight Abbot!" He stares blankly and sighs. He picks up the Blu-ray of Phantom of the Opera and walks back to his den.

———

"Thank you for coming on such short notice Ms. Lane."

"Of course." Helen tries not to panic standing in front of the Avenues' board of directors.

"We recently were made aware of an incident that occurred. You were in the hospital for two days correct?"

"Yes—"

"Now granted that it was a weekend and your internship wasn't interrupted, we are willing to overlook this. However, it causes some alarm the nature of your hospital visit. We were not told much due to confidentiality, but we were made aware you stayed on the psych ward floor."

Helen sucks in a breath quietly. *Shit. Shit, shit, shit.*

"Should we be concerned as to why you were there Ms. Lane?"

"No, sir."

"Do you have previous history of staying in any other mental health facilities?"

"No, sir."

"Can you safely say this will not happen in the future? Can we count on you to uphold the excellence that this school implements? We've heard nothing but outstanding things about you. It would be a shame to tarnish your growing reputation."

"Yes sir. Of course, sir. I will sir. You have nothing to worry about. This was a onetime thing. A slight hiccup but I'm better now. And I am more than willing to prove it by staying on with Avenues. If, you'll have me."

The board members take an impressed pause to think it over. Discussing with one another they pass on their judgments to the head board member. Helen swallows hard watching him look at her while hearing the whispered counsel. She takes a deep breath as he resolves to speak.

"Very well, Ms. Lane. But we do not want to hear any more alarming reports. This school will not tolerate a stain on its prestigious reputation. You may go."

"Thank you." Helen nods and quietly leaves. As she makes her way down to the first floor she sighs. She couldn't afford to lose this opportunity. Not now. Not after what she's been through and is trying to make up for.

Helen crashes into a boy with a laptop bag. She blushes and looks up to apologize.

"Oh I'm so sorry!" She tucks her hair behind her ear sheepishly. The boy smiles. Helen catches herself looking him over. Well he certainly isn't a boy.

"It's alright. I don't mind bumping into pretty girls. Do you go to school here?"

Helen blushes deeper, her hand making its way around her ear. "No, no I don't. I work here." They both laugh embarrassed. "What about you, do you go here?"

"No." He chuckles. "No I'm here for an interview."

"Oh, really?" Helen chastises herself for sounding ditsy.

"Yeah," he chuckles, "for the musical instruction of the high school."

"Oh I heard they've been meaning to replace the teacher. It was horrible how he got so ill. I hope he gets better. He seems old enough where that kind of sickness could kill him." Helen looks away and he nods.

"Yes, it's really sad." He frowns. He shifts his bag shyly. "I'm Josh, by the way." He puts a hand out to shake.

She reaches for it, "Helen."

"Sorry, bad timing after all of that." They laugh.

"No, it's fine." She looks him over again. *Hmm, cute.* Dirty blond hair that came out in short waves around his head. A neat light blue cardigan bringing out the stark blue in his eyes. A pair of tailored khaki slacks and decent dress shoes to match. *Not bad,* she muses. *Not bad at all.* She tries to breathe when she looks at his face. His smile dazzles her, and Helen suddenly feels goofy. Tucking a strand she moves to take her leave. "Well I hope to see you around."

"Well you will, if I get this job." He smiles crookedly. Helen fights the swoon and turns to the glass doors. She almost smacks into them as she watches him walk to the grand staircase. Her face burns from embarrassment as she ducks out into the midday sun.

Josh turns back to look for the dark haired girl. He smiles watching her walk past the glass doors. He turns back and climbs his way up the steps. The smile never leaving his lips.

Chapter Five

Carmen snakes his way around the dance floor. He wipes his nose removing the bit of white. His eyes scan over the crowd. A leering grin pervades his lips as he spots a slender red head gyrating to the house music. He backtracks to the bar and orders two drinks. Glasses in hand, he dances his way closer to the woman. Her friends size him up and back away. Encircling her, Carmen flashes his brilliant smile and offers the drink.

The woman raises an eyebrow but stops long enough to take the drink. She casts a seductive look over the rim of the glass. Carmen slides next to her. They dance closer and soon their bodies are grinding up against each other. She downs the rest of the alcohol and pushes into his pelvis. Knowing he has her he puts his hand on her hip and holds tight.

He whispers in her ear and they head off the dance floor. They sit at the bar staring at each other. Carmen hands back the glasses and asks for two more.

"You don't mind do you?"

"No, I could go for one more." She rubs the back of her neck relieving it from sweat. She whips her hair around and gifts him her "come hither" look. Little did she know, she need not bother. He was already game. While scrunching and playing with her hair she questions him.

"So, what do you do?"

Carmen knits his brows wondering if the relative truth would turn into a hurdle his charm would have to overcome. Reaching for the drink he cleverly spins the truth.

"I am the manager of this club." He waves his drink around the establishment. Before he can say anything else he sips hoping he doesn't have to. He peeks over at her.

"Wow…"

Carmen raises an eyebrow keeping his mouth to the rim waiting for the rest of her response.

"That is so—hot."

Relieved he casually smirks at her and puts the drink down. Absently the red woman rubs her neck.

"You look tired. Would you like to go somewhere *private*?" He leans in feigning concern. He risks stroking her hair back. The woman nearly swoons beneath his touch. The smile resurfaces and he leads her to the back of the club. They head up the stairs and into the private bedroom. The one hardly used that Evelyn had put in place after she won Carmen back.

Satisfied they were alone, he closes the door and sits the redhead down on the edge of the bed. He moves to the dresser and pulls out two glasses. He pours them both a drink and clinks two pieces of ice in each. Sitting down next to her Carmen hands her the drink. She smiles and takes a swig. Appreciating her tolerance for scotch he grins.

"So I've answered your question. So now, what do you do?"

"I'm a beautician at this fancy salon down in Manhattan." She waves flippantly. The last thing she wanted was to seem snooty to this hot guy.

"You're a long way from home." Carmen charms.

"Do you have a boyfriend, husband, or girlfriend?"

"Oh, no!" She chuckles nervously at her outburst. She strokes her hair. The way Helen used to. Carmen gulps back the memory and leans in to look interested. "No I just got out of a relationship. He was a real…jerk." She drops her gaze and nods.

"Well, his loss." He charms further. Holding her prisoner in his gaze. She pulls her hair back and begins to play with it shyly. All the while staring at Carmen hungrily. He leans back and waits for her to slowly heat up. He looks her up and down casually as her hair twirling becomes frantic. It isn't long before she jumps him and pins him to the bed. Attacking him with nips, licks, and kisses. Carmen chuckles through each assault enjoying the ride.

He flips her over onto her back and hikes her dress up. They grin expectantly at each other and he undoes his pants.

"Wait—" She stops him right before he slides in. They both look down. He raises his irritated gaze.

"Yes?"

"Protection?" She shyly requests.

"Oh." He rolls off of her and reaches around into the nightstand. He needs to refill this stash soon. It was getting pretty low. Carmen closes the drawer and climbs back on top. "Better?"

"Yes." She beams. He ruefully grins, shoves it on and thrusts inside. She squeals in surprise. Her bracing pitifully counters his reckless pushing.

The door bursts open and the red head jumps and screams. Carmen turns and grins refusing to break stride.

"What the hell is going on in here?!"Evey tenses her hands on her hips.

"Care to join us my pet?"

"What?" The redhead looks at Carmen in disgust, trying to get him to stop. He rams harder enjoying her resistance. Evey looks her over then slides her gaze back to him. She walks over and starts undressing. The woman's eyes widen in response. Evey strokes the redhead's face and lips. She shivers in response and looks curiously at Evelyn.

"She's delicious."

"Mhmm." Carmen manages between thrusts.

Evelyn finishes undressing and grabs her by the face. Her tongue wildly searches for hers and wins. The woman swoons beneath Evey's kiss and moves her hands from Carmen's chest. She leans back and reaches for the blond woman pulling her closer. The two women begin to moan and sigh as they passionately kiss. Carmen continues to pump fueled by the dueling sighs.

Evey tangles her fingers in the red tendrils as she pushes her breasts against hers. Moving slowly, she climbs on to the bed with them. Working together, Carmen maneuvers the red woman onto her knees and Evey slides underneath her. They resume their kissing as he pushes in deeper and faster. The red woman moves wildly against him, grinding into his pelvis. His eyes roll back as he loses himself in the rhythm of her hips.

With an arching growl, Carmen thrusts inside hard and collapses. He shrugs off of her and slops off the condom. With a disgusted noise he throws it into the waste basket. He turns to the two women undulating in the bed and rolls his eyes. Picking up his clothes he moves around the room getting dressed. He rakes a sweaty hand through his damp hair. He glances over at the bed and sees Evey taking control. Pinning her down and delving between her thighs mercilessly. She shoves two fingers deep inside and moves in tandem with her tongue.

Grabbing his jacket he scoffs and shakes his head. Without looking back, he opens the door and leaves. Closing it on the scene of Evey outdoing him once again.

———

Without even knowing where he was going, Carmen finds himself in the Upper East. He shakes his head as he sees the familiar streets. What was he doing? How could he even think Helen would want to see him? Well one way or another he was determined to see her. He turns the jag off FDR Drive and heads back to Glenwood.

Carmen takes a deep breath as he pulls into the garage and parks. He grips the wheel struggling to get a grip on his nerves.

"Hi Helen, long time no see—fuck." He slams his hands down at his stupidity. He licks his lips and rubs his thighs.

"I know it's been awhile but I haven't stopped thinking about you and I—"

"Shit." He sighs. His head drops and honks the horn. Startled, he snaps up and looks around. He fidgets for a moment and decides to hell with it and gets out of the car.

In the elevator he grapples with generic small talk and ice breakers. He panics realizing nothing smooth was coming out. Taking on criminals and seducing women no problem...talking to an ex...*yeah*. The doors ding open and Carmen hesitates. He jumps and jabs an arm between the doors as they begin to close. Jittery he makes his way out of the elevator and heads for her door.

One last sharp breath. His head hangs low as he softly raps. He leans against it as no sound comes from the other side. Three minutes pass... Five minutes... Carmen drops his hands and pushes off. He turns to leave and stops. Slowly he picks his head up and backtracks. He pulls out a key and opens the door.

What was so familiar and comforting now seemed so alien. So cold. Looking at the untouched furniture, the clean counters, and the barren walls Carmen sighs. What he wouldn't give to go back to this life. A husk of a life was all that he was living now. And it showed on these cashmere walls. Absently he strokes them like she did years ago when they first met at the café. He smiles to himself remembering how clumsy and foolish he had been then. How he spent so many nights hoping to see her there at Kaffe...

He snaps his head up. *No, she can't be.* Carmen runs back out of the apartment and makes his way back down to the lobby. A small dangerous bloom of hope splits open in his chest as he runs into the garage. He revs his engine and screeches out onto York Avenue. Heading back to FDR he makes his way to Kaffe. He yells out furiously when the traffic finally slows him down. His hands rake through his hair and yank hard.

Hope deflates as he finally reaches the Kaffe and struggles to find a decent parking spot. Defeated he parks a few blocks away and sprints his way back. Tears trickle down his cheeks as he fights the panic making his way around the corner.

Carmen huffs to a stop. He jerks out of the window and stands off to the side. *Helen.* There she is. He melts as he peeks at her. His heart leaps into his throat and plummets. She's not alone. *That should be me*, Carmen aches staring at the blond man standing next to her. This is what he wanted though. For her to find someone new. Someone who wouldn't break her heart like he did.

Gingerly he places a hand on the glass wishing she would look up just once. Pain spasms rock through him as he watches her laugh bashfully and tucks her hair. His heart nearly stops when they move closer and sit down. Parts of him that he had hidden deep surface and break in new ways he couldn't fathom. From the roots of his hair to his toes and out of the tips of his fingers, his blood sings stricken with refreshed grief.

How? ... How could he still say it was the right choice to pick Evelyn? Carmen was too selfish to think that this was right. To feel such pain so immensely and so completely knowing she was happy. And hating it. It should be him in there. That should be him stroking her hair back. Touching her face.

He had seen enough when the young man leaned in for a kiss. He slinks down the wall and slumps to the concrete. *Let me die here* Carmen laments. *Please*. His breath gives out as his mind recounts what he's just seen.

"No more. Please!" He grips his hair in anguish. But the pain from ripping doesn't ease the one in his soul. All those months, *years*, distancing himself, building himself up, and he was utterly broken again. He blubbers unabashedly as people walk by. Abruptly, he stands not wishing to be happened upon by her and the blond man.

Risking one last glance he looks inside. He sees them moving to leave. His heart puts up one last fight and pitters out. Black. The sneering gaze returns and Carmen shoves off and heads back down the street. His hand reaches into his jacket and grasps a knife. Whistling a tune he fiddles with the blade. Making his way back home.

Chapter Six

The laughter comes to a lull as Helen and Josh stand around her apartment. They both look into their glasses wondering what to say next. Helen didn't want to think about the awkwardness of the last first date she had been on. To take her mind off of it, she absently swirls her sparkling grape. The absurdity of the gesture makes her blush insecure about what Josh must think of her.

He looks over at her as she hides behind her hair again. She had been doing that a lot lately. He would think the date was going great and then—curtain. Josh tilts his head and moves off of the counter. Slowly, he makes his way to her. He puts his wine glass down and slowly strokes her hair back. Cupping her cheek, he forces her to look him in the eye.

"Hey." He smiles.

"Hi." She bites her lip and pulls back a little.

"No, no, don't pull away." He gently brings her closer to him. "I want to see your beautiful face."

Helen can't help but blush. After all these years, she still doesn't know how to take a compliment. She noticed just how *close* Josh was. *Kiss*-close. Judging by his face that's exactly what he plans on doing. But is she ready? Helen hesitates as he makes his move.

"What's wrong?" Josh pouts.

"It's nothing—I just. Nothing." She timidly smiles. He grins eagerly moving in for a kiss. Helen turns her face and sighs. "Ok, maybe it's just too fast?" Josh sighs as well and drops his hands. Stepping back he punches them into his pockets. "I guess now would be the time to tell you that I'm still getting over a bad breakup?" She shrugs bashfully.

Josh nods and leans against the counter. He picks up his glass, looks inside, and then places it back down. "Well maybe I should go." Helen slumps a little. She was afraid of this.

"If you think it's best." He walks up to her and gently nudges his fist on her chin. Helen doesn't know what to make of the cheesy gesture as she watches him walk past her.

"See you around kid." Josh saunters off with his hands in his pockets and heads for the door.

"Yeah see you at work—" it closes and Helen's face falls, "—Josh." She sighs and grabs her head. *Fuck.*

Just one of those times when you call up a friend and laugh about the botched date you just had. But Helen has no one to talk to. The only person she could ever talk to was—she hesitates and sighs. *Carmen.* She pulls out her cell and stops. Her thumb hovers over the call button. She shakes her head and decides to text instead.

"*Hey.*" She erases the message and tries again.

"*I needed someone to talk to and you're the only one I could think of. How's Evey?*" She sighs and deletes.

"*Hey Carmen, can we talk?*"

She stares blankly at the text. Acid leaks into her gut and churns her stomach as she contemplates sending. She couldn't take the rejection if he didn't answer. Or worse. If he did. A panic attack begins to rise and seize control of Helen. She sputters and gasps. Dropping the phone she hunches over and clutches her sides riding the spasms. She leans against the counter and slides down to the floor.

She had to get out of there. Glenwood had nothing left but grief for her. Helen struggles to her feet and grabs her phone. Pushing her hair out of her face she tries to collect herself. As she walks to the door she feels her resolve crumbling. She opens it and blunders out into someone's arms. She didn't care at that point who's they were. Helen lets go and sobs.

Abbot hums and coos as he strokes her hair. He slowly tries to get her to the elevator to take her home. Everyone was worried about her. He had finally tracked her down with her phone's GPS.

Helen looks up to see her old friend and weeps harder. She holds him tighter and buries her face in his chest. "I'm so lonely, Abbot."

"You're not alone little bird." He strokes her hair and fights a tear. His heart breaks seeing his little Helen in such pain.

Helen sobs harder knowing Abbot meant well. She loves her family, but family can't hold her at night. Family doesn't keep the darkness away. She loved her fatherly butler, but his arms weren't the ones she had hoped she'd run into.

It killed Abbot knowing he couldn't take the pain away with each tear he wiped. All he could do was be there for her the best way he knew how. "I've got the phantom waiting, with mocha almond fudge and mint chocolate chip. I hear there's some general Tso in it for you too."

He smiles down on her as she peeks up at him. He wipes the last tear as she manages to beam. "There now. There's my sunrise." He chucks his hand under her chin and grins. Helen giggles and smiles at Abbot. He always did know just what to say.

The next morning, Helen warily makes her way through the glass doors. Hesitating, she glances around looking for Josh. Wasting no time she makes her way to the stairs. Her heels clack as she jaunts up to the Lower School. Her eyes dart from side to side nervous of running into him still. Relief floods as she rushes into the classroom, closing the door behind her. She smiles sheepishly at her mentor and slowly turns towards the children. Their eyes were round with surprise at the sudden burst of the door and Miss Helen's crazed look behind it.

"Sorry," she waves meekly at the children. "Good morning children."

"Good morning, Miss Helen."

She smiles and nods finding her seat. Her mind drifts as the children resume their morning Mandarin lessons. She snaps towards the teacher when she hears her name.

"Miss Helen—would you like to take over class today?" Mrs. Everest raises a brow as she looks her assistant over. Her lips tighten as Helen fumbles to get out of her chair and retrieve the chalk.

It only takes her a moment to pick up what was being taught for the day. Scanning the chalk board, she notices a prevalent theme with the vocabulary. Shakily, she puts chalk to board and clears her throat. Taking a moment she clears her mind as well, struggling to remember the lesson plan for the day. Mrs. Everest coughs holding a paper out for her to take. Absently, Helen smooths back her hair and takes the vocabulary sheet.

Slowly, her hand draws the characters on the board. "我迷路了。有什么需要我帮你的？" As she finishes, she turns to ask the children to repeat the phrases.

"Wǒ mílù le. Nǐ néng bāngzhù wǒ ma?" The children drone in unison. Helen turns to them and smiles. Dusting her hands she asks them what this means in English. A few children raise their hands, while some snicker and whisper to each other. She turns to a little girl with bright eyes and a small mouth. Daintily she drops her hand and answers.

"I'm lost. Can you help me?" It takes Helen a moment to realize she wasn't actually lost. She risks a quick glance at the sheet and reddens. The vocabulary sheet was about problems and seeking help. She didn't even realize she picked those two phrases together. Dazed she looks at the child and nods. The troublemakers in the back snicker again at Helen's confusion.

"Zhè shì shénme làn dōngxī?" The class erupts into a cacophony of laughter. Helen blushes at her own ignorance and the childish feeling of embarrassment. The teacher's mouth drops as she singles out the boy who said it. She hides her shock when she looks to Helen and realizes she didn't catch the insult.

"Bìzuǐ! Liumang!" The little girl hollers back in her defense.

"Guǎn nǐ zìjǐ de shì, mèimei..." He draws out tauntingly. Her little cheeks burn and she shouts back.

"Cái guài! Pìgu." She huffs and slumps into her chair.

"Jane!" The teacher finally intercedes. Jane looks up hurt that she was the one to be scolded. "A lady never speaks this way." Her cheeks burned. Mrs. Everest looks to the back of the class.

"And *you*, Benedict. Apologize."

He grumbles, "Duìbùqǐ."

"Headmistress's office, *like!*" Her stern gaze burns into him as he scuttles out of the classroom. She turns to Helen and tightly smiles. She curtly nods as she resumes her seat in the corner. Her assistant gulps and regains her composure. The rest of the lessons go smoothly without a hitch.

When class is dismissed, Helen confronts her.

"What was *that* all about?"

"Oh, you know kids being—kids."

"What were they saying?" Mrs. Everest turns a wary eye and looks her over. Turning full frontal towards Helen she pauses.

"What? Was it that bad?"

The teacher breaks her gaze hesitating. When she looks back to Helen the hurt is already in her eyes.

"It was about you, yes. There was some swearing-"

"You teach swear words?"

"Heavens no! But you know how the smart ones are." She glances at the chalk board and frowns. "There's always a smart *ass* amongst them. And the Internet is just about useful for anything." She trails off into a hard gulp. Helen puzzles at her. *Okay?* Not wishing to pry, she collects her things and readies to leave. As she makes her way for the door, Mrs. Everest catches her by the arm.

"Don't let them get to you, Helen." Helen fights the urge to flinch as the woman's cold brown eyes bear down. Helen acquiesces meekly unsure how else to handle the awkwardness of the situation. A curt nod and the release of her arm is her reward. She tries to smile and exits the room.

Her hand struggles to smooth the worry lines when she looks up and starts. He walks right towards her with a crooked smile and his hands in his pockets. *Oh, I really don't have time for this*. Polite courtesy takes hold and she tightens a smile as he nears.

"Hey."

"Hi-" Her gaze wanders everywhere but on him. His smile droops and he runs a hand through his dusty blond mane.

"Look, I'm sorry about last night. I was a jerk." Helen absently nods, bunching her lips. Her eyes trailing over children going in and out of the music rooms. Her arms shift the messenger bag, shielding her.

"I'd like to make it up to you." He charms with a full smile, trying to meet Helen's gaze. She snaps over to him and blinks. Her cheeks flush at the intrusion and lack of hair to curtain her face. With no respite, she gives.

"How?" He grins as she finally looks at him.

"Well, how about dinner?"

"-dinner?"

"Yeah." He charms. Helen shakes her head from the dizzy haze and straightens back.

"Where?"

"Le Bernardin."

Helen fights back instant tears. Avenues and his warm American accent fades away as Helen tumbles back to that night. Le Bernardin, an exquisite French seafood restaurant Carmen took her one evening. It was the night she knew she could never love another man like him. He had taken her out just to spoil her. Helen was in desperate need of cheering. Her depression had started to creep when a call from her mother about her father frustrated her. It was the tipping point on top of all the planning for the end of the semester, and the crushing expectations of striving for a PhD.

Carmen brushed aside the open books and papers. He grabbed her clutching hands from her hair and held them in his own.

"Hey you." His warm smile gave way to the honey dew accent. She looked up, exhausted. For a moment, time stood still. She could get lost in those eyes if she really let herself. And for a moment she did. Her own closed as he caressed her face, letting a finger trace along her mouth.

"Hi." She answered in a husk. He chuckled and pulled her out of the chair.

"Let's go out." He beamed.

"Go out where? I don't really feel like it Carmen." Her voice threatened to betray the misery she struggled to contain. Her hair fell into her face as she bowed her head. He swept back her tresses and dipped down to look at her.

"Chérie, that is *exactly* why we must! Come let's get dressed. You can wear your hair prettily, and that perfume I like." A dark hungry grin slipped through his warm façade. Helen flushed catching it before it vanished.

"No." She pouted. She poked her lip out and whined. Carmen snapped up fighting the urge. He caressed her cheek.

"Helen, *please*, don't be so sad. I'll be forced to make love to you right here on the floor-" her eyes shone, "-ruining my carefully laid plan, and our dinner reservations." His eyes crinkled when she looked at him confused. "For me, ma chére, get dressed." He softly cooed. Helplessly Helen acquiesced, floating on a cloud all the way down the hall.

———

The jag turned onto W 51st Street. Carmen drove by Le Bernardin and found a nearby valet. When they made their way into the restaurant, Helen marveled. She didn't think she could ever get used to this. Her eyes raked over fresh orange roses and yellow orchids that graced each crisp clean table. The glasses made her want to cry, their crystal clarity adding a whimsical sense of sophistication to the atmosphere. Tea lights added the softest touch of romance, as they made their way through the dining room and to the second floor.

Fresh blush bloomed as the second floor spilled out in front of her. She hadn't the heart to even calculate what a place like this costs to keep running. Rows of round empty tables with more flowers and candles. Carmen grasped her hand and she looked at him, baffled. The faintest of smiles played on his lips. Deepening his gaze, he stroked back her fresh curls. He nodded to an alcove off to the side and led her to their own private table.

Helen fought back a swoon as Carmen pulled her chair out and sat her down. Flustered, she plucked the menu from the waiter and fanned herself. *Deep breaths, this is normal to someone like him. Be cool.* The more she fought for her nerve, the more she lost it. Especially, when he would look at her like that. Those glittering silver blue eyes transfixed her into a trance. How could anyone be depressed when they had someone like him staring at her so *deliciously?*

"Did you notice the mural when we came in?"

"Hmm?" She dazedly mused. He chuckled at her desperate fanning.

"The mural of the ocean waves behind the large crystal vases holding the crazy floral arrangements?" Helen halted and gawked at her boyfriend. *Wuh?* She couldn't believe a straight man had said *vase* and *floral arrangement.*

"Uhm-" She flustered, trying to remember. He chuckled again and grabbed her fanning hand. Stroking it, he gazed at her, willing her to calm down.

"Chérie, *breathe*." Helen gasped an inhale upon request and melted beneath his touch. They shared an intimate smile. Gently, Carmen brought her creamy hand to his lips.

"Merçi…" She gushed. Her senses collected, and sadness forgotten, Helen finally glanced at the menu. Her nose wrinkled. *Seafood, this is going to get interesting.*

"What's wrong mon coeur?" His brows knitted together, afraid his plans were about to fall apart.

"I don't—eat raw seafood… Or," she wrinkled further, "caviar." She gagged. Carmen's eyes widened in disbelief. A woman of such sophistication and learning he assumed her pallet was just as refined. His heart sank quietly realizing his *faux pas*. He snapped out of his befuddled daze, desperate to save the evening.

"How about the theme of the evening is 'trying something new'?" Helen looked up at him and bit her lip. How could she ever refuse that face? Seeing her cave, his hands resume their caressing. They locked eyes as he spoke.

"Let us explore our hearts as well as our taste buds tonight." His eyes crinkled with the crooked smirk. He knew he'd have her hooked when the accent flowed freely. Charmed completely, Helen couldn't help but nod yes.

"D'accord? Good, yes!" He beamed, nodding along with her.

"Well, what do you recommend then?" She glanced over the menu, feigning interest. Carmen cooly leaned back, clasping her hand tightly. He casually dipped his head down to the glossy paper in her hand.

"The entire list."

"That's helpful."

"That's our meal." Helen's eyes popped out as her mouth dropped open.

"What?!"

"Oui." Helen scoffed and looked around the private dining area. Her mind reevaluating and taking in the possibility of what he was insinuating.

"The chef, Monsieur Ripert, prepared this menu *special* for us."

"Bienvenue to Le Salon Bernardin, our private dining. Would we like to start with a wine? Or perhaps champagne for the occasion?"

Helen looked up at the suave waiter dumbfounded. Her wide gaze fell back onto Carmen in disbelief. Relishing her shock and awe, he gifted her another crooked smile.

"Oui, monsieur. The best champagne you have." Those crinkling eyes never leaving Helen's. She could feel herself suspended and weightless, held only together by the charm of his smile.

Helen didn't know what to make of the four courses of tiny entrées, as they made their way to their table. Each dish delighted and tantalized her imagination. And with each new arrival, Carmen smoldered and beamed. He took great pleasure in watching her eyes dance and her brows knit in wonder with each bite.

When the oysters arrived, he scooted his chair closer to her. His dexterous fingers strummed along her neck, caressing as the muscle and juices caressed her throat. He relished each moan as they bubbled to her lips with each lick and sip. Greedily, he let one hand drop to her knee. And as one continued to trace along her ivory skin, the other meandered down her thigh. Helen couldn't help but throw her head back as his grip emboldened her rising flush. His lips met beneath her ear, hungrily devouring her taste. Skimming his nose in her hair, down her throat and along her cheek, Carmen's arousal grew. His own dish forgotten in turn for the ivory feast before him.

Helen gripped the crisp linen as his hands delved further beneath her black dress. Soft sighs made their escape as her fork fell to the plate. His hand cupped her face, grabbing a hold of her. Just in time, Helen's head lilted giving in completely to his touch. A soft growl rumbles against her heated flesh as Carmen struggled to contain himself.

Someone cleared their throat forcing them apart. Chagrinned, Helen patted her hair down and straightened her dress. Carmen chuckled softly and turned to greet the older gentleman.

"Ah Chef! Bon soir!"

"Bon soirée Monsieur Bontecou. I trust everything was delicious *so far.*" They look down at their neglected plates. Carmen chuckled, rubbing the back of his neck.

"Well, monsieur, I must say it was quite *delicious.*" His smolder ensnared Helen for a brief moment. She blushed and turned to admire the view instead.

"And mademoiselle? How did you like your meal?" Helen's doe eyes fall on a supple smile. Embarrassed, she looked further up noticing the incredible hue to his hazel eyes. His light grey hair added a sophisticated flair to his well bronzed face.

"It was- an experience." She giggled.

"The view up here is breath taking monsieur-"

"Eric, please." The chef waived his hand warmly. Helen beamed. "Are you ready for dessert?" A wicked gleam danced playfully in his deep-set eyes. Carmen choked on his champagne and Helen flushed. Chef laughed light heartedly.

"I made it special for you, Helen." She looked up in surprise. Then she turned to Carmen. Her heart flew right out of her mouth.

"Okay," she shyly acquiesced. He clasped his hands together and grinned.

Helen turned to Carmen as Chef left and nudged him. His infectious laughter melted away her irritation and she joined in. They leaned against each other giggling. They didn't move when the divine chocolate art was brought to the table. Arm to arm, shoulder to shoulder, they fed each other. His excitement rocketed when Helen moaned at the decadence. His heart nearly stopped when she licked his finger cleaned, her gaze unerringly fixed on him.

"Check!" His voice cracked with his burgeoning flush. Helen rasped a chuckle as she wiped her plate clean.

Helen reels from the memory as she resurfaces from her haze. Looking around she remembers the crystal and the fresh flowers. Her heart plummets as she looks across the table to see Josh smiling. She ghosts a smile back and touches her hair. She clucks and sighs noting how absent minded she's been. Carmen's husky laughter lilts in the background and her heart breaks. When she turns around, it rockets up to her throat. She gulps and turns around painfully relieved it wasn't him.

"Are you alright?" Josh cuts off mid-sentence.

"Hmm?" Helen grabs her arm absently.

"You seem distracted, is something wrong? Should we go somewhere else? We can totally leave if you don't like it-"

"No- no it's nothing. It's nothing." She forces a smile and turns her full attention to him. He relaxes and beams back.

"I heard the food was great here. A little expensive, but hey," he pats his blazer, "I've got it." He winks and Helen snorts softly. Chin in hand she surveys the dinner crowd. A stark contrast to the serene privacy of Les Salons upstairs. Refusing to give into her bleeding her heart, she tunes into what Joshua is saying.

"-the students are great. I didn't expect to love coming to work every day. It's been amazing so far." He catches her staring and grins.

"Yeah, the kids are great. It's the bad seeds you have to watch out for. Hey do you know Mandarin?"

"Yes, why?" He looks up from his glass. She leans forward.

"Can you tell me what this means then? Zhè shì shénme làn dōngxī?" Josh snaps up from his drink and squints.

"Who said that?"

"This boy in my observation class."

"Uh huh-" he murmurs into the crystal.

"Well, what does it mean?"

"Depending on the translation, could either be *what rotten thing is this* or *what crap is this?*" He slides a glance her way, waiting. An irritated blush stings her cheeks.

"That little shit." She picks up her napkin and wrings it beneath the table. Unable to cheer her, Josh acknowledges the waiter with the first dish from the "Bernardin Tasting" menu.

"Ah, well this looks amazing. Albeit *small* but hey what can you expect from the French?" He laughs and rubs his hands together. Helen looks at him not knowing just how to react; to what he said or to what he did after.

The dishes were vastly different from the ones she had years ago. Everything was *cooked*, well sort of. Helen was grateful for the lack of fish eggs.

"I was thinking, maybe after dinner we could go to an art gallery?" Noting no visible reaction from Helen, Josh quiets. Feeling sorry for him she suggests an alternative.

"How about dancing? I haven't danced-in ages it seems." A sad smile greets her half empty plate as her hair slowly spills over her shoulders.

"Let's do it! I know a great place you're going to love it." They shyly beam at each other, settling into a comfortable silence the rest of the meal.

———

The thudding base drums right through Helen as they make their way into Pulse. She grins taking in the crazy lights and cliché fog rolling across the dance floor. She giddily claps and squeals as she takes in the retro pattern to the lit floor. Needing the escape, Helen throws herself into the beat. Twirling, gyrating, and rolling her hips. Josh's jaw drops as he takes in his coworker's rhythm and grace.

He jumps in next to her when the music changes to a hearty techno. Helen playfully shakes around, bewitching him with her hips. He slides his hands up and down her waist trying to keep up. She giggles and undulates until they fall on either side. Placing her own hands on top of his, she sways back and forth. He moves closer, feeling the beat thrum betwixt their pelvises. Helen jumps back, dancing out of his grasp. She smiles wickedly shaking her head no. Josh throws his head back with laughter and nods. He stops and watches in awe as she moves about the floor. Dramatically, he clutches his heart and spins around. Helen doubles over with laughter and picks up the pace.

Seamlessly, her body falls back into the ballerina groove. Joshua's eyes widen as her muscles ripple beneath her smooth skin. Dubstep permeates through her twists and arabesques. Eventually, Helen can't distinguish music from muscle. The swift precision of a cobra, with all its venomous grace, Helen loses herself completely to the tumultuous sounds.

On the stairs, Carmen watches her. With each writhing undulation, and swift pop of her limbs, his heart constricts and balloons. Strained tears give way to a ravenous salivation as she hypnotizes him. Stunned in place once more by his goddess. It felt like death, standing there paralyzed by the torrid of emotions. The violence of which was parallel to none.

His eyes peel as he finally sees who she has come with. That blond bastard again. His heart thrashes around, screaming and raging for her. And for his blood. Carmen snaps out of it. He looks at the couple, his eyes wet with shame. With his tail between his legs, he returns to the office. Dying once more.

Helen sways and twists letting her body move supernaturally slow and inhumanly swift. Her mind buzzes and swirls and the colors spin before her eyes. She sighs and swings her arms out and above her head. She dances into a frenzy soaring off of the high. If only this feeling could last forever-she'd never need to crawl inside a bottle again.

Evelyn enters the club from the back and makes her way to the back stairs. Looking out into the crowd like a queen greeting her people, she smiles. The smile freezes and disappears completely when she sees Helen. Her eyes peel at the young blond man near her, watching. She harrumphs and smirks darkly. *Carmen!* She quickens the rest of the way and swings the door open. Her heart flutters and steadies when she sees the scoundrel in her chair. He looks up and locks her gaze.

"How is my naughty boy?" She muses.

He growls menacingly and erupts from behind the desk. She giggles as he pins her against the door.

"Shut up." He whispers darkly.

————

Helen sighs when the music takes on a dizzying throb. Josh leads her to the bar and they laugh. She orders a water while he sits dumbfounded, recounting what he had just witnessed.

"-wow."

"What?" She chokes out from behind the bottle.

"What was *that?*" He juts his chin to the chaotic floor.

"Oh," she blushes, "it's been a *really* long time since I've had fun. And even *longer* since I've danced." She smiles wiping the dribble from her chin.

"Well, we've got to change that!" He slaps his hand down on the counter. "How about we try to come here at least once a week?" Helen gawks at him mid gulp.

"Okay," he guffaws embarrassed. "What say we try for at least every two weeks—or whenever you feel like it?" He smiles. Helen eyes him warily, lowering the bottle.

"Uhm-"

"We're friends right? Friends go dancing together!" He grins encouragingly. Helen considers it beneath her poker face.

"Okay." She innocently beams.

"Yeah?" She nods excitedly. They high five and he turns to order a drink. They lock eyes as they greedily gulp down. Helen could use a friend. She didn't really know what it felt like to have one. Other than Abbot, there wasn't anyone else. Her face falls a bit, and she catches herself dragging him back to the dance floor.

Bodies writhed on the floor and upstairs behind closed doors. Lust swirled in the hot, muggy, salacious air. Hunger rises in the blue of a young man's eyes, and abates in the belly of a dying pale Frenchman's. Their desires locked and twisted in the bramble of a toxic love affair. Both their hearts and sights set on the one woman they can't have. Their minds blinded to those caught in the cross hairs of their misguided fixations. One woman's innocence melts in the sway and lull of a familiar dance. Another's lost to the bitter cold of resentment and old times past. Both waiting to be saved by the one they desperately love-not wanting to admit to the pain he so expertly exacted.

Part Two
Chapter Seven

Helen was on her way back from her weekly AA meeting. She was three months sober, and loving every minute of it. She couldn't wait to get home to Josh. She beams to herself at how much he encourages her. From those shivering nights of withdrawal to the close calls at the bar, Josh was Heaven-sent.

If he hadn't been there for her—she didn't want to think about it. She finally had someone she could rely on and actually trust. No thoughts of spiraling were getting in the way of that today.

She closes the door with a sigh. He was waiting there with a kiss and a cup of Earl Grey. She squeals beneath his lips as he hands her the tea.

"Hey."

"—hey." She mouses, biting her finger. She didn't know what it was about him, but he brought out the school girl in her. She wasn't sure if she liked this or if she was just being a chicken shit. Either way, she was going to enjoy the ride wherever it took her.

"So, I was thinking after such a stressful afternoon, we could take a picnic in the park?" Josh gently massages her shoulders as he whispers in her ear. Helen could just melt. She whips around and perches her hands around his neck.

"Yes!" They giggle as their foreheads touch. She nuzzles the tip of her nose against his and smiles. "—nose kiss!" Josh chuckles and closes his eyes.

"Nose kiss." His husky laughter bats the base of her throat making her flush. The haunting echo of Carmen's dances between her thighs. She whimpers, fearing the masochistic pleasure. The deep dark coil snakes its way up and spreads like wild fire. Desperately, she tries to stifle the moan that threatens to ruin a perfectly good afternoon. Her mind screams at her to be strong as her nose breaks the kiss and skims along his ear.

"Honey? What about the picnic?"

"Fuck the picnic."

"Wait! The tea—shit!" Helen's laughter tinged with fear drips with a menace Joshua was unaccustomed to. She peels his clothes back once he disposed of the cup. Hungrily, she inhales his rising sharp scent as she moves to overtake him. She claws her way down his back as she nibbles down his chest. He tries to fight the oncoming soft cry, only to be bowed backwards over the couch. She scratches her way down until she rests between his thighs.

She forces his legs open leaving red marks down the sides. He arches with a hiss as his cock twitches. Helen purrs darkly as she grabs a hold of him. A violent undulation of pumps and twists stir and torture Josh. Wickedly, she licks her lips and plunges down over him. She moans as she sucks and pops, taking him in deeper and deeper. Her captive cries out unsure of how to respond.

Her eyes gleam with salacious triumph and bites down around the base. She gets up before he can and hooks a finger in her mouth.

"Oh." Her eyes widen. Her lips forming the perfect "o". She steps backward in chagrin.

"I've been naughty haven't I?" The finger trails down her chest and stops at her pelvis. She rushes him taking his cock by surprise with her reaffirmed grip. There it is, the delicious high.

"Too fucking bad." Her laugh was sinister as she hurls him back over the arm of the couch. Her grip slickens as she moistens her hand. Her other shoots up and plunges deep within him. She pumps as his wretched moans escalate. She pulls her hand free and unwraps the other from his cock and stands.

"We can't be having that now can we?" She plucks her panties from the pile and gags her boyfriend. Back on her knees, she waits for him to beg for mercy. His dulcet torture swirls around her reddened eyes as she takes him back into her mouth. As his agony fades she smiles. Popping him back out, she stands and slaps his thighs until they're red.

"Keep your hands to yourself!" He whimpers.

"—you know what? Let me fix that." She walks away and comes back with a mask. Grabbing him, she massages and coos.

"Wear this baby," she breathes down his neck. Her tongue trails down his face and back again. With a quick jerk and a tug the bondage hood was secure. Josh thrashes until Helen's ivory hand snakes its way down his body. Satisfied by his submission, she goes back to work. She moans as her mouth tightens and moistens around him.

She sucks harder, willing him to fill her with the poison she needed. For the shame that she craved. And for the misery of degradation and oblivion. The savory incandescent beauty that was her sadistic desires—letting it come to a head, bursting into a cataclysm of pleasure, and then crashing into inevitable pain. Like clockwork.

A free hand makes its way beneath his shaft and slowly massages new whimpers out of him. He squirms and tries hard not to touch her. He was almost where she needed him to be—to release the beast. He whimpers and moans through strained pipes. His body shoots up and down over the arm. Helen smirks around his shaft and bites down once more. He hollers and doubles over. In a crash, Helen falls to the floor. Her widen gaze drinks in the monster struggling to get free.

His eyes met her in a wild craze. His nostrils flared as they fought to catch breath the mask had steadily choked off.

"You crazy bitch, now you're going to get yours." The dark husk laden in his voice sends shivers down her spine. *Showtime.* Her face freezes in mock horror as he stalks closer. On cue, she stumbles away and takes off down the hall. Hidden in the darkness, Helen tries not to giggle. She hears his feet pad down towards her.

While she waits, her spine tingles with a new sensation. Blood lust. A hunger grows and overtakes her delicate sensibilities. The burning rage she's kept welled up inside, seeps through the cracks. Her head rolls from side to side as her eyes flutter. She licks her lips with anticipation as he makes his way to her. Helen purrs as he grabs and pins her to himself. She moans as his hands make their way down around her waist, up around each breast, and close on her neck. A finger pops itself into her mouth, forcing her lips apart.

Her own rake through his hair and pull him closer. Craning her neck, she beckons him to taste her. Josh pauses, taking her in, and sinks his teeth. She licks her lips as he endeavors to break skin. The burst of pleasurable pain sears her vulva as the blood trickles out. He turns her, ramming her against the wall. He pins her pelvis to pelvis, and plants a sanguine kiss. Her fingers drag down the back of his head, leaving trails of red. She shivers as her blood boils with the urge to rip him apart. The rage and sadistic lustful impulse coil her muscles and she pushes him off.

Surprise glitters in Joshua's eyes as he falls backwards. Helen's guttural laugh throws him further. She perches on his chest and looks down at him.

"Oh no, no, no, darling. Don't move. I want you— just. *like. this.*" She grazes her teeth along the base of his throat and down over his chest. Her hand reaches down and grabs his cock, pumping it back to life. She jumps on and begins to rock her hips. As their morbid rhythm quickens, Helen's nails strike his flesh feverishly. His growing screams spur her on as she tears at his flesh with teeth and nail, drinking him in. Devouring his pain, drenching herself in this dark revelation. This is what it means to truly cave to the dark swirl that ever pervaded her mind. To become a monster—and frighten the one just beneath the surface.

She rocks him harder in their cradle of filth. Her arms stretch out on either side of her as if in ascension. Head rolling, eyes fluttering, Helen was exercising demons she had long thought put to rest. Flashes of her father in the dark gave her whiplash. Her head thrashes as she picks up a ferocious pace. Trying fruitlessly to fuck the visions away. Her rage flourishes as her hand strikes his cheek. She roars, furious at what she was doing, and at the man who had ruined everything.

Helen digs her fingers into his shoulders as she pounds down upon him mercilessly. She looks down to see him staring up at her in confused wonder. The ferocity of her feral glare collapses his resolve. Shutting his eyes, he holds on tight.

"Open your eyes." The menacing honey drips from her husk. Bewildered, he does as he's told and gazes up exposed.

"You will watch, like I had to watch." Before Josh can speak, her hand wraps around his mouth and clamps down.

"No matter what I do, keep your EYES open!" Wide eyed, he nods. Helen purrs and removes her clasp. Her salacious rocking turns thunderous as her body undulates, rippling with heat. Her dainty fingers mockingly tweak her nipples and she bites her lip.

"Is this what you men want?" She careens down at him, tauntingly playing with her breasts.

"For us to do all the work?" Her hands slide up her throat and into her hair and she moans garishly. "For you to just sit back, relax, and get fucked while we put on a show?" She pulls close and coos into his ear.

"But what about what *we* want? Hmm?" She holds his gaze as her nails find new purchase in the hollow of his throat. She pushes in and relishes the ensuing gagging noises. She clenches around him and rocked. Her fingers pulsated in time with each thrust she makes with her pelvis.

"Do you like that *baby*? Do you love it when I fuck you? Does that feel *good*?" Helen moans as he starts to choke. She fans her fingers over the base of his neck and squeezes. Her laughter darkly echoes as she tilts her head back and grinds. Satisfied with the sadistic fix, she clenches and pumps her way to orgasm. Josh's hands shoot up and grips her hips. They slither off the couch and onto the floor holding on tight.

Her mouth pops open as her fingers wrench her tresses. Her lover's face scrunches with effort, but his eyes never left his mistress's. He comes as he listens to her piercing cries of torrid ecstasy. They collapse into a bloody heap.

———

Helen beams as she turns the corner. Her face glowing from the week she's been having. With her head held high, she cracks the door to Kaffe. She waltzes up to the counter, smiling as people squeeze by her.

"Chai tea, please."

"-What happened to Earl Grey?"

She reluctantly turns to her side, eyes wide at the lilting accent. She couldn't believe it. He spoke to her like it was only yesterday. A yesterday filled with promise of a jaded tomorrow. How dare he speak so casually after three years of silence? Of *torment?*

And what can she say to him after the endless nights of ruddy, bleary-eyed misery full of pain and darkness?

"Are you fucking *kidding* me?" Her hands wring in the air. Carmen startles out of his charismatic gaze.

"Here you go ma'am." She swipes the cup off the counter and swiftly bolts for the door. Carmen dashes after her. Abruptly, she stops and turns to him. He juts to a halt.

"No, you're not getting off that easy. I want you to suffer." Carmen didn't dare move for fear of losing her once more. His mouth finally closes and he waits for the oncoming storm.

"There were nights I nearly died for thinking of you. My breath gave out and I swear I didn't want to take another for fear of having to *feel* again. To acknowledge the pain waiting after the asphyxiation. Terrible nights tossing and turning waiting for your face to fade away.

"And when waiting it out didn't work-" Carmen cringes waiting, "I drank myself half to death. I didn't care anymore…whether I lived or died. My own mother found me in a puddle of cheap wine, face down! Do you have any idea how mortifying that is?

"-Don't answer that!

"My mother's hired help put me on suicide watch for months!

-Carmen winces.

"Do you know what it's like waking up in a hospital not knowing why?"

Actually chérie- he rouses himself and catches the change in her voice. "Car-men," her eye involuntarily twitches as her throat dries against his name, "I hope to *God* you do not ever look for me again." She tries desperately to swallow the bile of anger. The crackle of blood lust, moments away from erupting.

He can't help himself, "Why is that, chérie?" The smallest voice shutters out from behind the cracking walls around his heart.

Helen's nerves ignite as her muscles spasm beneath the blazing flesh across her cheeks. Her blood beats wildly against her skin, as she ignores the urge to fight or fuck him. Carmen's eyes widen in bewildered fright. He falters back, raising his hands in cautious surrender.

"I'm sorry to have disturbed you, mademoiselle." He bows deeply and Helen turns and sails out the door. Slowly, he stands upright aching in her absence. How could he have lost her for the *second* time?

Where was it written that lightning's disastrous strike should make its mark twice upon *his* heart? Catching himself as he doubles over, he stumbles into a chair. His hand flies to his chest and grips tightly. He slams his other down upon the table. Letting it ball into a fist. He steels his breath as the plasma cools in his veins. His eyes glaze as they fix on the door. And his heart is hardened once more. As if in a trance, he stands and makes his way out. With one hand in his pocket, and the other fiddling a switch knife, Carmen makes his way home. Whistling his favorite tune.

———

Josh walks through the door and finds Helen on her second full glass of merlot. *Shit*, he laments. Her last fall off the wagon was embraced with a light hearted moscato. That was three months ago over the brats at school. But the deep dark pull of merlot is too great for a recovering alcoholic. This only meant one thing.

"Shit…" He drops his bag and gently crushes her against his broad chest. Helen's hands fly up and she nestles, breathing him in deep. The wine completely forgotten.

"Mmm…" Her face buries into his cashmere and she drifts.

"Do you want to talk about it? He whispers into her hair. She surfaces and smiles.

Catches me every time. She looks at him warmly for a moment. "No," she shakes her head, "not right now." He smiles and nods pulling her close.

"Alright. Did you still want to go to the Met?"

"What are we seeing again?" Josh gleams.

"—Macbeth." Helen squeals and clasps her mouth.

As she watches from the balcony seats, Helen chews her lip. Lady Macbeth was in the middle of her blood lusty monologue. Josh shifts next to her and catches her eye. She feigns a smile as her mind storms beneath the surface. He pulls her close and settles back into the play. Was it her or did his arms feel *alien* all of a sudden?

Her mind drifts to the Kaffe incident. Of all the things to say to him! She sighs and shakes her head. *Idiot.* Then again, she hadn't planned on ever seeing Carmen again. He did look delicious though. Helen's distraught now. She doesn't understand what it all means anymore. She hadn't really been religious or superstitious, but after the seemingly random run-in with an ex at an abandoned haunt, she wasn't so sure anymore. Failing to see the would-be sign, she huffs.

"I know! I wish Macbeth wasn't such a pussy either." Josh whispers. Helen forces a small knowing laugh and sinks back into her thoughts.

She shouldn't have cared anyway. She didn't need him. She didn't need any man for that matter. Helen snuggles into Josh's ever inviting arms. *But boy, did it feel good to have one.* Who was she fooling? Josh was no Carmen. She hates herself for comparing them, but really can't help it. Especially, since they've been doing strange, albeit frugal, versions of what she used to do with Monsieur Bontecou. Helen rolls her eyes, remembering the thick Occidental accent. A dull ache follows right after. *Damnit, that accent.* At that moment she would've given anything to hear it.

Panicking with her wishful thinking, she leans over in her chair. Scanning over the balcony, maniacally, she tries to spot him. Satisfied, after the third go-around, she leans back, deflated. And relieved. There's no reason to indulge her fading masochism once more. It wasn't worth it. He—wasn't worth *it*.

Suddenly depressed, Helen shifts in her seat. "What's wrong babe?" Josh turns towards her, fully concerned. Sweeping back a flat-ironed tress, Helen fidgets with how to answer. She cops out to save the evening.

"Nothing. Nothing." She does her best little girl smile and hunch of the shoulders. Her palms pushing down on the trench between her thighs. Warily, he eyes her unsure how to proceed. Like a good boyfriend, he brushes his fingertips across her cheek making his way to her hair, tucking it behind the ear. His thumb caresses her creamy skin and he smiles comfortingly.

Without breaking her gaze his tone takes on a honeyed sincerity, "He's not worth it you know?"

"I know." Her gaze threatens to drop and he catches her. Holding her by the face he closes.

"I'm serious, Helen. No man, or no *guy* for that matter, is worth your heart breaking again and again. Now, I love you, and I'm here with and *for* you. Live instead of dying on the inside at the end of the day. Live just once, in the moment—with me.

"Marry me."

Helen's lower lip escapes its bond as her eyes saucer. His mandible tenses as he apprehends her answer. Clasping her hands over his, she answers, "Yes." He relaxes and cracks into a cheese. They kiss with a lingering seal of the deal.

"I love you." Helen floods with frailty in her soul as she says the three words she thought she'd never say again. But here she was, living in the moment.

"Congratulations." An older woman adorned in nouveau riche garments whispers. The couple turn to her and thank her through giggles. Josh lets go of their clasped bond to fish into his pocket.

"I'm so glad you said yes." He whispers with a husky chuckle. Helen blanks out of shock. She blinks.

"I planned the whole thing—leading to this." The ring dim in the theatre glints. The perfect princess cut three diamond set. Tears burst down her cheeks at the sheer perfection of the engagement story. Her hand moves forward waiting for it.

"It's—perfect." Helen mews as she studies her new finery.

"I measured your finger while you were sleeping." Josh points proudly. *Albeit* creepy, Helen still chuckles.

Is this the fairy tale ending that so many girls looked for and few women actually found? It seemed like it. Helen can't remember a time when she was happier. So *this* is love. *This* is bliss. A glittering promise of the moments yet to come.

But despite how deliriously happy she felt, there was the small ache panging deep within. This was supposed to be her perfect moment

—with Carmen.

Chapter Eight

Evey looks out the window of her condo. Taking another puff of her slims, she broods. This was getting *too* boring. Carmen was doing everything she wanted him to, but he still didn't love her. She didn't understand. He was supposed to love her. And now if he wasn't fucking her, he was out fucking shit up. She missed the old days when it was just unruly philandering and blow. At least he was fun *then*. But *why* didn't he love her?

Carmen walks into the room and greets her placidly. Like a puppy fighting love sickness, she turns to acknowledge him anyway. He rifles through the mail on a nearby tale. She exhales and extinguishes the cigarette. She sits down in the oversized chair and watches him. She knows better than to just start talking. They never have anything real to say to each other. She watches him walk about. A patient jungle cat declawed and confined. Her restlessness gets the better of her and she moves to speak.

"Do you love me?"

"What?" He turns, tepidly annoyed. Evelyn's heart recoils.

"Do you? *Really* love me?" She delivers evenly.

Carmen growls for a few seconds. Ten terrible seconds. Without breaking her hawk-eye gaze, he delivers evenly right back, "I'm. Still. Here. Aren't. I?"

Feeling the little girl in her rile up, she stifles a shoulder shift. Carmen's eyes zero in and peel.

"What!" He snaps.

She tries not to flinch at the bitter resentment laced with indignance seething from his voice. All she ever wanted was for him to love her and for things to be as they were in Marseille. Was that so much to ask?

Risking her fragility, she opens up. "It doesn't *feel* like you love me." She can't help the ensuing pout he was sure to take to as pure manipulation. On cue, his eyes roll with a growling huff. He storms towards her. Noting her subtle flinch, he calms and drops to one knee.

"Of course I do." The patriarchal pity bleeds into his words; her ears not missing a single drop.

"But—" she sulks.

"But *what?*"

She hesitates, "—Do you love me more… than *her?*"

His muscles freeze, fighting the onslaught of wincing, throat constricting, and bile churning at her words. His hesitation shifts and with as much conviction he can weakly muster, "Of course I do." Fighting a final twitch, he grabs her hand in consolation. His voice unctuously dripped with honeyed sympathy.

Evey bats back the tear threatening to spill. Her intuition keen on his well hidden disgust. Her throat tightens as she plays the part of the doe-eyed Juliet. Mustering a heartbreakingly cheery smile, Evelyn pretends, if only for the moment. He buys it and gently pats her hand, ghosting a smile back. Seeing the pain in her eyes, he tries harder. His hand steadies as it brushes her flushed cheek. He thumbs it as his other sweeps behind her ear. Freshly cut bottle-red hair met his hand where the tangle of blond used to be. He leans in and gently kisses her creased lips. She loses her resolve and her hands fly to his face pulling him in deeply. Tears stream down her face. Wiping one away, Carmen takes them for relief. But Evelyn *knew* better. She had considered reneging her vendetta months ago. How could she now when he didn't even respect her enough to tell her the *truth?*

She stops the kissing and looks at him. Thumbing his cheek she excuses herself. "I have some work to do, mon chér."

"D'accord—mon amour." He takes her hand one final time and plants a gallant kiss. Her heart flutters at the small gift of sincerity. But her mind rebukes and she stands to take her leave. There's unfinished business to attend to. And this cold dish of revenge has stood for too long. It was time to start the *real* fun. As she turns to him on her way out, they catch each other and smile. A shared smile of bitter pain and despair so palpable, so rich, that both pairs of eyes mist as the door closes behind her.

———

What is it about little miss priss that Evey doesn't possess? She grimaces at her obvious youth. But *besides* that, *vraiment*, what was so great about fucking *Helen?* As she recalled, there was a certain someone she couldn't hold onto that Evey had no problem taking. Her face falls further. Surely she wasn't more experienced. And surely she wasn't *nearly* as flexible. Evey chuckles at Helen's short comings. She noted not an ounce of confidence in that girl. And she had all the sexiness of a bewildered frightened *petit lupin.* Why was Carmen *so* infatuated with her then? She growls at the failing insight. If only she could be but a fly on that little trolip's wall—slowly it dawns on her. Flipping out her phone, she presses 9 and slides it to her ear.

After a beat, "It's time." Classic Evey smirk triumphs her face as she ends the call. Picking up her pace, she heads to her car. *Just one quick stop to Pulse,* she muses, *and then off we go.* If the love she's after isn't going to stand the test of time, she's going to have some fun on her *tour de vivre*. So much to do—so little time. She had a kidnapping to plan and a heart to crush. But in the meantime, while she waits for everything to fall into place, she's going to fuck the pain away.

————

Days pass since the call. Evey lost track of how many men she went through since then. There was that first night where she (frankly) outdid herself. After slipping into something sexier (a black catsuit with fetish spiked heels and a matching belt), she gathered her wits.

The first one was easy. She simply needed to flash her "come fuck me" eyes. The second took a bit more finesse. This was a *two-dick* problem and she was intent on finding a solution. She convinced the first meal to sit on the side lines while she bagged the second.

She sauntered slowly out onto the dance floor. If Carmen doesn't want to appreciate this, she mused, then somebod*ies* else will. She signaled to the DJ to spin her man-catching tune. As the beat fell into full swing, Evey's hips began to undulate. Posture on point, her stilettos in full show, she moved like the serpentine queen she was. Eight pairs of hungry eyes gleamed with salacious appetites as she hit every move. As the song came and went four out of the eight had made their way to her. Out of the four only two seemed ready to party.

As a new song came on she danced with each. Then the final test. She groped and kissed one and turned to make her way to the other and did the same. When the first took his leave with disgust, she chuckled. Like once before, she walked the youth to the bar. When a lull in the music settled in, she moved in for the kill.

"How would you like to be in my ass tonight?" She purred. The twenty something stood shell shocked.

"Parlez-vous anglais?" She jested. Still, he held his mouth agape unable to speak. Evey moved in closer, casually unzipping until her mighty cleavage could breathe.

"I *said*, 'voulez-vous coucher avec moi, ce soir?'" She trailed a finger down. Encouraged, the hound grabbed a hold of her waist and pulled her against his bulging reply.

"Oui," was all he could manage with his flat American accent. She put a gentle hand between them to unload the catch.

"Ah, ah, ah, only if you know how to share mon chér." His confusion was met with a sweeping hand pointing off to the side. With a beckoned finger, Evey summoned a dark rippling urban early thirty something forward.

"This is Kareem, and he'll be your partner for this evening." She chuckled at her stewardess impression.

Kareem put his hand out to shake the likely white suburban reject's. Confused, the younger lad did what was expected. He looked to Evey, brows arched. "So you get down like *that?*"

"You know them cougars—they get freaky." The black man nodded knowingly. Evey blushed coquettishly on cue.

"Lady in the streets, but a freak in the bed!" The buzzed youth hooted and high-fived his newfound bro. "Hey man, I don't cross swords and I definitely don't pitch or catch—"

"Don't sweat it man, this lady here is all about the *DP.*"

"Ah…" He nodded feeling his unspoken desires unfurl. The result of too much porn.

"Shall we gentlemen?"

"After you." They managed in unison.

"And who said chivalry is dead." Evey gushed with a girlish shrug and crinkled nose. They smiled until she turned to walk, their eyes glazed as they caught sight of what they would be partaking. She led them to the spare bedroom her and Chad had once frequented.

"Hey, uhm, you seem like a really nice lady and all, but I can't get down without a rubber."

"You mean these?" She flashed a box. He lit up like a Christmas tree. "But you won't be needing these." The white boy was about to object when she carefully unzipped and stepped out of her bondage wear. She turned to face both of them. Their eyes took in every voluptuous inch.

"—Because *you* will be in my mouth." She stared him down until his objection faltered. She lifted into a feline grin and turned to her dark chocolate. She picked up the box and meandered over.

"As for you—"

"I don't need that shit. I like to feel my lady all the way." Evey arched a brow, dramatically slipping them from her fingers. Her hands perched on his chest and purred.

"Then I leave it up to you big daddy, which prize to claim." Her devilish grin spurred him on and he pulled her in by her waist. Evey was spun around and placed chest down on the edge of the bed. With one hand pinning her, the other freed himself from his stone washed jeans. Without further ado, he rammed inside, eliciting a dark hoarse moan.

After a few strokes, her *duexieme garcon* grew restless. She propped herself up and locked into place. Tauntingly, she faced him letting her mouth fall open. Receiving the invitation, he bounded and leapt onto the bed, dick out. He slid in working up a lather. When she was nice and greased, he grabbed her by the cheek bones, and pumped. Evey's jaw slackened and let him in deeper.

Her eyes fluttered backward as they moved in perfect harmony. Back and forth. Back and forth. Their very own forty year old something see-saw. When both had worked up a good stroke, the younger looked up.

"Dude—" when he finally caught his attention he raised his hand. The other rolled his eyes, but grinned meeting his hand halfway. White boy was thoroughly encouraged after that. He looked back down at Evey and stroked her hair back. He hunched and leaned into his stroke savoring. Emboldened, he took it a step further.

"Look at me!" He gruffed. Evelyn's eyes catapulted open. When she didn't readily obey, he wrenched her chin upward. "Yeah, right there, just like that. You suck that cock. Good little dirty bitch."

Evey didn't know what to make of this imitation of American pornography. Especially since his hand had made its purchase on her taut eyelids. It was one thing to be lost in the dark revel. It was another to have to witness her own demise. Not wishing to spoil it, she let the little girl out to play. What was left of her innocence was shredded through the gaze of her molester. A sticky swirl of masochism colored her own red. She greedily sucked and tongued the flesh penetrating her soul.

The black man gave into his own demons and ripped out of her dripping. Gripping her hide, he split her open a new one. Evey choked with surprise at the switch up.

"Yeah choke on it. You fuckin' choke on it!"

He shoved violently down where her tonsils once resided. Not wishing to be outdone, dark chocolate picks up his own rampageous pace. The see-saw was being incredibly sawed, and Evey was right there on the edge. The small divide between pain and pleasure. She tried to readjust her palms and was abruptly slammed into submission.

"Stay down bitch." Gruffed her rear-end partner. The other grunted in sadistic amusement. For a moment, Evey felt out of control. It was *fantastic*. She would definitely treat these boys to a meal afterward. She bucked and choked as fluid escaped her eyes and mouth. A salivating sore of a mess, pumped in motion. Her ass reddened and her throat strained. Pain she had come to love.

A swift flash of her fathers from France came to mind. Her eyes grew wide unable to shut either out. She remembered her biological father back in Toulouse. A vision of her *pere vrai* walking out on her mother and down the street to Mme. Loupe. Her *mere* crying and drinking herself desperate, waiting for Monsieur Canard to arrive. Images of peeking behind cracked doors, hearing her mere trying to get over her pere with a different man every month. Evey remembered meeting her papa in Marseille. How he took her in and showed her how to be a skilled thief and a seductive assassin. How he eventually took advantage of her twenty year old youth. The last real image of shame Evelyn saw last brought a tear to her eye. Her, 24, on her *rotules* sucking off her dear *papa* beneath his desk in his boudoir.

Evey swallowed back the tears. Not knowing any better, white boy took his encouragement in stride.

"Oh she's thirsty after all the sweatin' she's been doin'." A shared laugh between the scoundrels ensued.

"I'll feed her," he pumped emphatically, "while you see to it that her thirst gets quenched."

"Right. Come on grandma, it's time for your *warm milk.*" An arrow sang a chill right through her heart. *That hurt.* She bucked up regardless, bracing for the finale. With one last gasp of air, she asphyxiated; letting the dark flood mind, body, and soul.

"Don't go ragdoll on us now." Evey came to hearing the black man's cohorsive purr. She gulped for air, losing concentration. She tried to get her bearings, while both picked up their paces once more, holding on tightly. Her spine suffered as her backside was rear-ended and her neck whiplashed. Her gag reflex tripped harshly and she struggled once more. Amidst the inner maelstrom, she heard a caucus of growling roars. Then all at once, she was skewered, Sam-n-Eric style. Suspended in an instance, her ass and mouth flooded with Release. She blacked out for only a moment. The delicious *petit mort.* Like the good girl she was, she did as she was told. Swallowed.

Both men pulled out and teetered respectively backward.

"Wow." Breathed the one slumped on the bed.

"Shit," managed the one off of it.

They collected themselves and dressed. She hadn't moved by the time they were done.

"We didn't kill her, you don't think?"

Mr. Chocolate moved closer and nudged her, "We're gunna head out. Are you good?"

Evey surfaced from the black fog for a moment to groan her annoyance.

"Cool." Quietly, they picked their way out of the room. As she resubmerged she heard white boy ask him-

"Do you know how to get outta here?" If she had the strength, she would've rolled her eyes. She shook her head and rested. Face down, ass up, Evelyn found peace at last.

The nights following weren't as fulfilling as that first. So like a crack addict, she tried new ways to get her fix. One evening was spent in a bar lavatory on her knees with a cock in her mouth that eventually made birth in her ass. Another spent tied up in the bedchambers of some shady BDSM practitioner. He was a little *trop* zealous for her taste. The rules governing that underground lifestyle irritated the shit out of Evey.

After only two weeks though, the luster wore off. All that perspiringly glitters isn't gold. She'd hate to sound like a cliché but that was exactly what she was turning into.

———

She finds herself in a SoHo bar, smoking and sipping white wine. She recants the other day with detached despair. This inevitable plummet that ensues her masquerading leaves her reeling. Her head slumps against her ash flicking hand and she lets her eyes glaze over. *Quel désastre.* She was a disaster. Too much of a mess to be beautiful in some tragic *triste* way. Too proud to own up to the fragility within. She wasn't even having fun anymore- which bored her most of all. But what burned her soul was how much she felt like that little twerp in the coffee shop. The day she thought she secured her own *happily ever after.*

Evey wasn't supposed to feel like her, she was so *dreary*. Her *sang française* was accustomed to misery—but Helen wallowed in it. Swam around and took laps. Will Carmen love her now that she too was just as drenched? The idea sends a sweet sickening bloom of hopeful poison through her veins. A brief sadistic peace is broken by the onset of reality and her surroundings bleeding through. She drags a long one hoping to stifle the tearful gag of despair.

What the hell was it about that damn *souris pathetitque?* It can't be all on looks—so what is it? She itches her twitching temple and puts out the slim. Which is chased with a swig. Her mind wanders back to her introspection. She was surely stronger in spirit than her and definitely wiser. Evey had been convinced that young men wanted *women* not mice. Helen was barely out of *l'université*, ce n'est qu'une enfant! C'est incroyable!

She scoffs before downing another swig,

"—fucking child."

Taking comfort in the cathartic sentiment, she sighs. Maybe that *was* it. She had become "the momma". No longer fresh, desirable—but a nagging pestilence. One that hovered and demanded. Her shoulders slumped at the intoxicated epiphany. *Mais tien!* She'd spent the last few weeks fucking her way through Manhattan! *Mais bien sur* she was desirable! The victory was short lived as the resounding fact remains. She was desirable to all but *un*.

"Carmen." She groans into the bar top. A plum of heartache threatens to topple her reserve. Her nails dig into the side of her face. Fruitlessly trying to get a grip. When none is found, she spills over caving once more.

He was supposed to be her *l'amour vrai*, her *bonne fin*. She would've done her pessimistic parents proud had they still been alive. Her lot in life was no better than where her mother ended up. Working, for nothing but for the sheer feminism of it all, alone, with no one to love at night when the day was done. A bitter smile gapes upon her chin at the irony of ending up nowhere different. But, wishing her way back in time isn't going to make the present any better. Because *maintenant*, she has nothing. Nothing but the pleasure of her own company.

Who needs men anyway? She bitterly balks. Who needed a man she couldn't stand to be around—when she couldn't even handle herself alone? *Loneliness.* The driving force for so many. For Evey, it's her few favorite vices that keep her going. But she can see so clearly now why so many stopped at nothing to drive an impenetrable wedge between themselves—and nothingness. That sinking desolation, revenge and a broken heart can't keep away for long. Like a rubber band snapping back unto itself. A brilliant star trying to outrun the inevitable devastation. In the end, even Evey had to embrace the cold dark truth. You can't love someone else, until you learn to love yourself. And like so many of the human race, she just couldn't quite love herself enough.

An unassuming married man sits down beside her. "Let me buy you a drink?" She lifts her head and looks over. Taking in the stranger, she brightens.

"I'm only drinking white wine." She taps a finger on the glass with a lazy smile. He thinks on it for a moment and looks at her triumphant.

"I was thinking *champagne*." Evey creeps into a devilish grin. She raises her glass in cheer. *Finally, a gentleman.*

—If she couldn't have any real *fun*, she was going to get *even*. And so the pair drank in each other's company over pink champagne.

Chapter Nine

Night creeps in across the floor as Carmen blanks at the ceiling. His sweeping lashes struggle to bat back the oncoming tears. Backburned images from the Kaffe torture him. There aren't enough tears for what he's done to her. But all the same, Carmen believed he had earned a night off from his American veneer of masculinity. Not that he wasn't opposed to abandoning the conditioned practice all together, but, he was in the minority.

But men couldn't possibly be *this* stupid? All that show of chest puffing and dick grabbing was for other men. Universal signals of conformity. *And savagery.* Women don't even seem to care about all of that. They simply wanted to be seen and heard as a person with kindness and respect. Only the broken ones got off on prehistoric biochemical signaling. Which it seemed, bred more stupid.

All real women wanted was to be loved tenderly, and cared for after they married. To be able to live fully and freely without the need to check herself. Without the man getting in the way. To be able to stand on her own two feet, with a partner right beside.

Why was this so difficult to grasp? The paradox of it all. Carmen racked his brain but came up empty. He hadn't the faintest. *Peut-être,* if the Fates are kind, Helen (after extensive closure) can illuminate him.

Helen's no longer his to love freely. Having to face the totality of this, the fire in him gives out. The smoldering embers left seems only to suffocate him.

Moving as if sludge through sand in the world now. Propelling forward by the blind instinct to live. The word "pain" doesn't even begin to describe the phenomenon produced by his pulmonary black hole. He's held together by his impulse to stay busy and his hard liquor. But when mind, body, and soul are riddled with devastating shrapnel, nothing ever truly holds.

He reaches over to the night stand for his glass. Mechanically, he takes a sip. The tin man finally learned what it meant to feel with his heart. With no Dorothy to thank. For it isn't her face alone that haunts him, but the countless slain in her name. And the several that weren't.

I wish I had told you. The tears pierce as the nightly ritual begins. *I wish I had told you!* Would she have believed him? He gulps another sip down. Every part of him aching to be near her. To soothe her. To calm her. To earn back her forgiveness. He wonders what she's doing *maintenant.* Probably giving the most intimate part of herself to that boorish cad. Who is he anyway? It doesn't matter anyway. Helen made it very *clear* she wanted nothing more to do with him. Carmen's renewed hopes for redemption deflate once more.

Sex and murder disgusts him now; since they were only morbid walls caging his heart. Vice and sin permeating Pulse just depresses him. No more mirth for the swarm of people dying to be loved in all the wrong ways. There was a time when he would've pretended to enjoy himself among the filth. That time had long died since Helen. There was something so pure and untainted about her. Maybe it was the naïveté she possessed. Or the blush that spread warmly across her cheeks when her delicate sensibilities were challenged. *Présque,* it was the breathtaking charm to her unassuming air.

Dreams of her loveliness perfume his vision as his heart beat wildly for her. *Helen…* he closes his eyes and sweeps a hand through his hair slowly. It was now almost a perfect impression of her caressing touch. When the moment ends, he sighs. He's afraid of what will happen when the high wears off completely. The time it took to perfect also took away from that *haut parfait*.

He fills his lungs, reclining back against the headboard. He glances at the clock and looks once more to the ceiling. Now's the time to calm himself and keep it together. Evelyn'll be home soon. Then there was her to consider. She was getting harder to read. Did she really love him—or was it *Memorex*? His head reels from the Evey who wept weeks ago, to the Evey fucking everything in sight. She was a creature far beyond his comprehension. She was as likely to love as she was to stab him. *Again.*

Carmen churns over to the side, grimacing into the pillow. He sighs, dropping the tension from his shoulders. It isn't much of a mystery anymore why women could be so crazy. He, and others like him, made them out to be. He rolls onto his other side and shields his eyes. How many times had he looked at Evey with secret disgust? Outright contempt? Caused her so much pain just by being so dishonest? How could he have been such a coward to let Helen go just so they could both live? Why hadn't he *fought* for her? Why the fuck didn't he run out the door that day?

I never wished for any of this. I never asked for this wretched life of mechanical customs and robotic people. The more he thinks on it, he realizes a great horror. His beloved childhood book had, in some regards, come true. Machines without feeling, walking through life apathetic. The haves and have-nots sharing in their insipid indifference. And here were two women on the opposite ends of the spectrum of *feeling.* Both felt pain he had inadvertently inflicted. Both had hearts and minds that were strong but weakened in his presence. Both had given *leur tout* just to be with him and keep him around. Both *loved* him. Had loved him. And where one chose to weep the other chose revenge. But, it seems now, even Helen has succumbed to the bitter scorn of her counterpart. It was a lonely thing realizing he was all alone now. He wasn't fooling himself with all of the philandering. He simply wanted to fuck the pain away. And by simply doing that, he fucked over the only two people who truly cared about him.

But it was Helen who had shown him the way through the darkness. She had made life worthwhile. *Magical.* Made the sweetest love, so gloriously breathtaking. *A goddess divine.* She was lit from within when she wasn't too busy hiding her flame. She was his safe harbor; his lighthouse. A ship left on stormy seas could rest easy by the white of her light.

Carmen floats on the foggy bliss as his mind carries him away once more. A small measure of peace gifted to him by his goddess. His heart strings steel against their clippings as reality sets back in. He may feel tortured. He may feel pain. But he would be damned if he ever truly let Helen go. Evelyn could never take her away like that. She had touched his soul. All the demons in the world couldn't touch him for the sake of his love for this angel. His tragic weeping angel. And her pain still burns him cold. She had handed back bloody what had been unjustly ripped from her chest in the first place.

If he's ever going to make amends to the women in his life, he needs to first mend *la premiere Coeur.* Evelyn walks through the front door quietly. Carmen slowly rouses from his bedroom to meet her in the hall.

"Salut."

"—salut." She steers past him and into her room. He follows behind blindly. He steps in as she undresses.

"Pardon-moi." He throws his hands in surrender. She starts and quickly covers herself. Carmen blushes, chagrinned.

"Desolé…"

"It's alright." She snaps an awaiting top up off the chair. She holds it over her chest and glares. "Do you mind?"

Surrendering for good, he gingerly recedes. He closes the door deflated. Hopeful, he waits for her to step out into the hallway. He back peddles and follows as she makes her way out.

When she reaches the end of the corridor, she turns on him. "What do you *want* Carmen?" Her eyes peel shrewdly.

"Puis-je parler avec toi, s'il te plait?"

"Why? We have nothing to say to one another."

"Presque, Je t-il-fait juste."

"I don't particularly care to right now."

"—s'il *vous* plait? Je vous manque."

She scoffs and rolls her eyes, "You can miss me all you'd like." She pivots on her heels giving him her back.

"I'm bored with this. *Au revoir* Carmen."

"Wait!" He leaps forward catching her arm. Thinking better of it, he lets go and slides in front of her. Beneath her withering gaze, he beseeches once more.

"Please." His eyes drink in hers—giving her his all. Something softens within her and she sighs.

"—what?" She breathes exasperated. His stomach jumps into his throat, forcing him to choke on his Adam's Apple.

Cautiously, he leads her to *le canapé* and sits down beside her. Taking one hand into his, he gently strokes with his thumb.

"Je sais—" she eyes him.

"—I know I've hurt you irreparably. But, if you believe there to be some way to forgive me, you would make me the happiest man alive." Evey's lip falls slightly. Taking her shock in stride, he presses on.

"Evelyn, I care so deeply for you. In the past, I was dead on the inside, *long* before we parted ways. By the time of the fight, my heart had frozen over, my soul in ashes. I was a withering man of 25.

"I should have never taken advantage of you. I would blame youthful ignorance, but I didn't change as the years passed. The horror and shame I feel for having tossed you aside—*comme si tu etais rién*. And for all of those years I have wronged you; violated your dignity, your soul, *et ta coeur—ma chérie, je suis très, très, très, desolé*. Please... forgive me?"

Silence hangs heavy as his words settle around them. Gingerly, he genuflects before her. She gasps in spite of herself.

"Evelyn Marie Bijou, *veux-tu... me marier?*"

Her eyes saucer as he removes a wooden box from his pocket. The lid drawn back, they feast on the bouquet of jewels inlaid on a platinum ring. Amethysts, rubies, and emeralds dance in the light as they play into flower petals and butterfly wings. A tear springs to her eye as she looks up at him.

"Yes." She tearily nods.

Relief floods him as he pushes the ring back upon her finger. And with a cliché inspection, she beams at her upturned hand. *What I always wanted.* She clasps him by the face and pulls him into a kiss.

'It's beautiful!"

"*You're* beautiful."

Their eyes lock into a dreamy standoff. Carmen smiles brilliantly and she staggers a breath. For a moment, she forgets herself. The tears drip bitterly as her heart re-hardens.

"Oh *Carmie,*" she purrs as she embraces him. Caressing him, she mews softly in his ear. "I wish you would've done this sooner." The sweet poison seeps from her lips.

"I know chérie, I—"

A swift blow to the head sends him to the floor. Evey sighs, patting her red cockatoo do with her ringed finger. She pulls it away and it looks it over. Canting her head, she clucks begrudgingly.

"The man does have good taste though. *Une si gaspillage!*" She steps back from the pile of Carmen and strokes the face of his attacker. "Bravo, mon chér."

Her heels clack with finality as she makes her way down the corridor.

"Let's end this." She muses darkly. Revenge was sweet. And Evey was not one to say no to her razor sharp sweet tooth.

Chapter Ten

HOURS EARLIER

Helen couldn't believe she was finally engaged. She looked down at her hand again in disbelief. Josh held her proudly by the waist as they left the theatre. She chuckled at his James Dean expression of satisfaction.

"—I have to ask."

Helen looked up from opening her car door.

"Are you *deliriously* happy?"

Her brows knit together confused at his redundantly random question. He walked back around and took her by the hand. Gently, he moved closer and looked deeply into her eyes.

"Well? How are you...*Mrs. Darcy?*" Helen had begun to swoon. He caught her by the chin, redirecting her gaze.

"My Pearl? How *are you?*"

"I'm—fine. I'm fine." She whoozed with a shy grin. He ran his fingers through her hair and thumbed her cheek. Josh moved next to her ear.

"*Je vous aime.*"

"You know French?"

Josh chuckled, "*Oui madame.*" He casted his gaze off into the distance. Helen couldn't believe it. Why didn't he speak to her before? Maybe because he was saving it for this moment? She blushed and bit her lip.

One swift hand reached around and planted a cloth over her mouth. Her fright buckled as she went under.

Helen awakes to the darkness. She feels around helplessly only to recoil. A rising panic creeps up as her eyes struggle to adjust. Nothing but black. Her panic redirects her attention to the stinging numbness around her wrists. She rubs them struggling to recall anything.

A few minutes tick by and she snaps up to the sound of a muffled voice on the other side of the wall. She puts her ear up against it, cringing at the frozen surface.

A groan? What the hell is going on? She panics more hearing the sound of scraping metal. Chains? Biting back the spring of pain she gets to her knees and moves about the icy darkness. The bleak outlook of the situation sets in as Helen fails to find a give in her confinement. She weeps, slumping back down onto the cold floor. Where the fuck is Josh? *Oh that fucker.* Her teeth chatter as she pulls her knees up under her. She props her chin on them. Bitter tears frost her cheeks. She burrows her face despairing her poor judgment.

Fear seizes as a cacaphone of harsh cries fill the air. Even behind the thick freezer door, she can tell someone is being tortured. She tries not to go into shock when the cries are interrupted by a new sharp sound. The abrupt yanking of what seems like chains. A tear washes away as she silently mourns the poor soul. And prays to God she isn't next.

Chapter Eleven

ONE HOUR EARLIER

Blinking, Carmen opens his eyes only to feel chains about him. Alarmed, he comes to quickly, rattling. Evey emerges from the shadows with a dark husky chuckle. He strains against his restraints growling beneath his breath.

"Why are you doing this?" He seethes.

"*Because.* I enjoy it too much." She moves closer. "You're sexy when you're tied up like this." She looks him over. "All pissed off and *helpless.*" Her hand snatches his chin out of the air. She hisses playfully. Chuckling, she steps back relishing the moment. Carmen's head falls in weary defeat. Sweat trickles down his shivering body. Barely containing the rage.

"—you, are *beyond*—a cunt." He huffs.

"And *you*—sound really winded. Why are you so out of shape? You barely shook yourself!" She laughs.

"How am I supposed to feel when life leeches from me, anytime you are *near?*"

"Oh Carmie, don't talk like that." She saunters up and squeezes his cheeks together. He tries to pull away but her nails dig, catching him. His shoulders cave as the exhale gushes out betwixt her fingers. With mock disgust, she clucks and smears it all over his face.

"After all this time," she rubs her fingers together, "you still don't know how to keep your spit in your mouth." She shakes her head and steps back. Just for good measure, Carmen manages some spittle on the floor.

"Why you little—" she rushes him, taking aim to his groin with a knee. A harsh groaning cough escapes his defiant lips.

"Maybe now you will learn some manners."

Helen finally bangs and scrapes against the ice box. Evey turns to acknowledge it with a wicked smile.

"Ah, it seems our guest of honor, has finally awakened." She rubs her hands together and turns to see Carmen's horror stricken face. She curls into a wolfish grin. His neck bends to the weight of defeat, as his and Helen's fate are revealed. So his past had finally caught up with him. And *this* was retribution.

Through deep jagged breaths and heavy lids, he manages, "*Why?*"

"Because you haven't paid in full just yet. For what you've done to me."

"S-s-stabbing you in the back? For leaving you?" He weakly lifts but gives out suddenly. His body suspended in chains.

Evelyn laughs icily, "Are you fucking *kidding* me?" Carmen winces at the familiar echo. She waits for him to lift again. When he steadies, she begins.

"My whole life, I waited for a man like you." She clucks in disgust, "If that's what I can even call you. *Un homme*, if only. Just a boy with a big dick, which by the way, you don't know how to use at all.

"—you took advantage of my loneliness. My need—my desire to love and be loved. You swept me up with your charm and courage, and then threw me away with the rest of *la famille*, like garbage.

"What's worse is you expected me to just roll over and *take* it.—

"No I didn't, I knew this day—" a swift slug to the gut cuts off his pedantic plea. She fixes her suit and pats her now black Marcel waves.

"I wasn't finished. Interrupt me again…" She trails off with a menacing gaze. Barely able to raise, he groans with effort trying to stomach the pain.

"Who did you think I was, Carmen? Some mobster's whore who didn't think past her own nose? I knew *exactly* who you were. That's why I even took a liking to you. You were so pitifully arrogant and ignorant to a fault. I felt compassionate enough to want to help you see the error of your youthful ways. Hoping against my better judgment, that once I saw you through, you would do the same for me.

"You were my hero in the dark filth that *Papa* felt so readily to drop me in. Do you know what it's like feeling unloved, ugly, and so insecure that you find yourself on your knees almost every night trying to win the favor of a man you saw as your father?

"Do you?!" She rattles his chains seething in his face. Too weak to flinch, he gazes at her. Waiting.

"Of course you don't," she hurls back with disgust, stepping away. She grabs her face as her heart breaks in front of him. Turning back to him, she lets him see the wrathful tears.

"You were my *hope*. My chance at a happy ending. My salvation away from that place. And you left me.

"YOU LEFT ME!" The tears pour as she rages on. Carmen buckles. The tragic epiphany settles in. She did love him. The way he loved *Helen*. The pain moves him to wince. Helen! She was still in the freezer! He wearily looks over to it, the tears betraying him.

"Aww, are we feeling for your true love? It's your fault she's turning into a Popsicle…" She lowers her voice, her face falling. "You were my true love, Carmen."

"My one true love." She turns, eerily calm. A dagger reveals itself and he stifles a gasp. Each decided step makes his heart race as she points it at his heart. She laughs bitterly seeing the alarm in his eyes.

"Oh silly boy, I'm not going to kill you. I'm going to kill *her*. Death is too good for you. I want you to know exactly what it feels like to have your ever after ripped from you—as you have so ripped it away from me."

She rushes him and digs into his flesh. He grunts not willing to scream and alarm Helen. A salacious gleam darkens her face as she begins to carve over his left pectoral.

"I always wanted to get matching tattoos like these Americans do."

"E"

"V"

"E"

"Y"

By the time she finishes her name he's screaming in agony. The blade digging in further and further with each progressing letter.

"There. Now we will *always* be together. Even after death." She wipes the metal clean with her tongue. Luxuriating the taste. Carmen's stomach rolls and he winces at the pain.

"Shall we bring out lover now?" His eyes round at the realization. "I'll take that as a yes." She turns her back on him and meanders to the ice box.

Helen's eyes flutter and droop as she fights hypothermic shock. Periodically convulsing she tries to black out. But can't. This definitely wasn't like how they explained in books. Jack Dawson always looked like he didn't have a chance when he hit the icy Atlantic. And she was *surviving*. And fully conscious of just how freezing it was. She blinks as a door opens on the other end. She hadn't even tried that side. The familiar clack sends fear shivering through her. *Evey*. Before she can even protest, she's hoisted to her feet grimacing in pain. She gasps when her eyes finally adjust. There he was, bloody, broken, and chained. A new sliver of pain snakes down.

"Now that all of the party guests are here, let's begin!"

"Almost everybody—" From the corner of the shadows emerges a blond henchman. Helen faintly twitches seeing Josh appear. His voice isn't the only thing changed. His whole appearance seems more *sinister*. A true chameleon. His golden locks were buzzed off, and a stark blue suit was in place of an inviting cardigan.

Helen limps in Evelyn's embrace. All her psychology meant dick in the face of this sociopath. She bought it, *all of it*. Her ring finger burns with no reprieve. Evey jerks her upward ushering her forward.

"Would you like to do the honors, *brother?*"

"Oh, I would be honored, *sis.*"

Helen's head begins to throb as she changes hands. Josh drags her over to some rope strung over a meat hook. Dazedly, she watches him bind her and raise her arms over her head. There's nothing she can do but endure the fire consuming her body. He steps back admiring his work; then leers in Carmen's face. He growls and jolts the chains. Josh stands back, chuckling by Evey's side.

"You!"

"Yes, *me*. I'm surprised you recognize me, *brother*. Well, P90X can do that. And a healthy dose of juicing." He chuckles.

"God damn you Andy!" He roars. Helen swoons. *His name isn't even Josh?*

"Tsk, tsk, that's hardly complimentary coming from an orphaned noble. I expect more from you." He wags an admonishing finger. Carmen's rage consumes him as he fights to break his chains.

"Well I think we've kept Helen in the dark long enough." He saunters up and grabs her by the chin. Disgust lumps in her throat. "I'm sure lover boy has shown you his scars hmm?" He finally forces her to look at him. "Did he ever show you the one I gave him?" Not satisfied he scares a reply from her chapped lips. He grins and sneaks a look at Carmen. "Right here." He turns her face and licks. She whimpers in spite of herself with fresh tears. He drops his hand, and snakes it between her legs. He stage whispers in her ear, "and here."

Carmen's vision bleeds a fiery plasm. A menacing growl rips from his chest and Andy turns to him, peeling his lips back. He steps away from her and jeers in Carmen's face.

"Shall we finish what we started all those years ago, *mon frére?*"

"Unchain me and find out." The blood boils beneath his skin. Evelyn and Andy's eyebrows raise in unison, amused by his words.

"Not part of the plan, *cheri.*" Andy pouts mockingly and steps aside.

"You—were the one who fought him when he wanted to leave Marseille?" Helen manages between breaths.

"Yes, little dove, I am he." Carmen growls his way.

"So what happens now," she sardonically rasps.

"The end—" Evey cuts in.

"You're doing all of this just to kill us?" Josh moves back to join Evelyn's side.

"*Sis* has always had a flair for the drama." He chuckles, and skims his nose along her neck. She closes her eyes and revels in it. Helen hurls completely undone.

"Ugh! Great now I have to clean the floor." She clucks in disgust. She walks up to Helen and smacks her. "Don't do it again." Knowing she's going to die anyway, Helen risks a loogie in her face. Earning a swift kick in her stomach. Had she anything left, it would've been on the floor then as well.

"I'm so sorry Helen." Carmen blubbers.

"What this? I can't feel a thing, I've been freezing and burning for the past few hours." She grunts.

Evey chuckles, "Who knew a little torture would gain her some pluck." Andy pulls into a smirk, his eyes menacing.

He walks slowly up to her and raises his hand to the knot on the hook. Staring her deep in the eyes, he takes her down. His fingers make their way up her sides until they hit her face.

"Ah!" Helen starts at the razor sharp finger armor bracing her skin. Drinking in her terror, he lingers down her cheek. Not willing to give him full satisfaction, her eyes lower and she tips her chin upward. Andy chuckles darkly. His hand clasps tighter, digging until ruby spills, and wrenches her chin down. Helen can't help but cry out. Evey lifts into a feline smile.

"That's enough *frère.*"

"D'accord." He bores into her soul once more. Satisfied the fight in her was quieted, he rips the point from her cheek. She whimpers and droops as he places her back on the hook. Carmen's growls and rattling chains fade in and out for Helen as she loses consciousness.

Andy steps back holding his gaze. Tauntingly, he raises his finger to his mouth. His tongue laps all around the point letting his eyes close savoring the moment.

"*Tu es mort.*" Carmen rumbles evenly.

Andy bows, canting his head, "*Aprés vous.*"

"Enough." Andy looks to Evelyn awaiting her command. She turns to him and strokes his chin. "Let's leave these two *love birds* to some privacy. They are entitled to their last goodbyes." She smirks at the pair and heads for the restaurant cellar door. Andy gifts them with a ghoulish grin and does the same.

When sure the door is firmly shut, Helen huffs.

"Well, this is twisted." Carmen breaks down again leaning against his chains in embrace. She weakly looks to him.

"I thought one day I could ask for your forgiveness. And now, I—" His blubbering takes control.

"Woah, shh," she rasps and winces, "Don't—don't cry. You're supposed to be the man, and if you cry well then…"

"Yes, chérie, we really are that fucked." Helen eyes her surroundings with renewed fear. She slumps. At least she was by his side. She stirs when the chains scrape against the brick wall.

"I miss the days when most of my troubles came from the other side of my bedroom wall." The last resolve breaks and Helen cries at his small confidence. She shivers and winces crying and aching around her fresh wounds, and her old ones.

"I love you." She whispers letting her sorrow consume. He strains to turn to her, his heart swelling. And just as it swells it bursts knowing that those three little words had to have come at the worse time.

"Helen—"

"—I never stopped loving you." Realizing she wasn't stirring, he reluctantly rests against his restraints. "I failed you. I failed you as a man, and as your knight in shining armor.

"I was supposed to be there for you—*with you* always. I was supposed to protect you." He chokes on the tears.

"You should've never eyed me in the café then." Carmen's head drops at her croaking reproach.

"I deserve all your wrath and more. I had been dreading this moment for fifteen years and—"

"The ballet..." Helen softly laments her naïveté. He weakly nods. If she could, she would've bitten her own lip at her own stupidity. He had tried to protect her then, and she belligerently fought him.

"Well fuck a duck." Carmen pitifully chuckles at her attempt at pluck.

The door swings open and the horrible duo reenter with new toys. He shutters at the sight of his fate and takes one last glance at his beloved. She had weakened at the sight of them as well.

"I hope we gave you enough time. It was too delicious not to let it go on for as long as it did. Helen, darling, I think in another life we could've been friends." She chuckles. Helen looks up at her with a confused grimace.

"Evelyn, in another life, I would've never known you."

She juts her bottom lip in mock contemplation and smiles. *"C'est vrai."* Fondly she strokes the dagger in her hand. Helen stutters a sigh knowing this was it. There was one last thing she could do before it was too late. "Now this will only hurt *a lot."* She rushes with the blade aiming for her gut. A choking gurgle escapes Helen's lips as the metal meets flesh. Evey's grin seals the deal as she twists. With a gasping breath, Helen pulls Evey closer.

Planting a sweet kiss, she whispers, "I forgive *you,* Evey."

Startled, Evelyn wrenches backward. Her mouth agape, she takes in the mousy thing. Helen manages a look down to the sound of a slow drip. Her crimson droplets were cascading down the silver and onto the concrete floor. Before she fades she hears her knight roar in agony.

"Your turn," Evey mews menacingly. Carmen lifts his head and spits one last time in front of her.

"Hmmph," her eyes peel as her lips curl back.

She storms him and grabs him by the chin. Forcing it open, she runs the blade across his mouth. Making him taste his beloved's precious garnet right before he dies. Taking the blade she presses it against his throat. His eyes blaze with a defiant fire, never leaving hers. Meeting the challenge, she grins and runs it slowly across. Andy moves closer, standing on the other side of her.

"Goodnight *brother,"* he sweetly drips.

Just then, the cellar door bursts open. Evey retracts in surprise. Andy turns and sneers at the tall silhouette.

Moving swiftly, the man apprehends Andy first, bludgeoning him without hesitation. Evey screeches and hurtles after him. He side-steps letting her slash through the air. Using the same blunt object he thuds her in the spine, sending her reeling. She turns, limping and livid. Again, she tries to sail towards him. He drops the phone just in time. He catches her midair by the wrist. Using both of his own, he twists wrenching her arm. The blade clatters to the floor. She tries to wriggle free, sending her limbs into a frenzied attack. He grunts trying to dodge while they both stumble backwards. Reluctantly he slams her face forward against the brick wall, rendering her unconscious. Her screams cut off with a wet smack. He drops the body and rushes to Helen.

Carmen's eyes widen in disbelief as the old man hefts her off the meat hook. His mouth closes as he watches him caress her and attempt to staunch the bleeding.

"Little bird?" He strains a whisper. He rips his dress sleeves and forges a makeshift tourniquet. He sweeps her hair back frantically.

Flashlights flood the room as a group of officers and EMTs make their way in. Firefighters reach Carmen and begin to break him loose. Confusion gives way to relief as he drops to the floor, finally free.

The medical team move in on Helen and Abbot. After assessing her wounds they gingerly pluck her from his arms and carry her to a stretcher. He springs to his feet and follows calling after her. Surfacing from the black, Helen peels back her eyes only to have them sear from the light. Hearing Abbot's voice, she brightens and then moans at the fresh pain.

"Daddy?" The little girl in her voice cracks his heart and he rushes to hold her hand.

"I'm right here Helen. I'm here, I found you. You're safe." She manages a wincing smile.

"Abbot…" She drifts. She resurfaces with an adrenaline panic. "Carmen!" Her eyes dart maniacally. He shushes her and strokes her face. Then, she hears the familiar Occidental roar. Carmen fights his way through the uniforms and weakly stumbles to Helen's side.

"I'm right here baby. I'm right here. I won't leave you." He grips her bloody hand and raises it to his lips. She smiles peacefully and closes her eyes once more. Remembering herself she reopens them.

"Good," she rasps, "cuz you *owe* me."

"Anything chérie!"

And as the stretcher makes its way through the dinner rush, Helen slips.

EPILOGUE

A crowd ornate and blissful gather round on a sunny spring day. Their fine garments and cheery demeanors just right for the occasion they're about to witness. Just then, the music sounds and a creamy skinned bride with raven hair walks down the aisle. And even though they are all so happy to see her walking in her fine silk beach dress, the only one stunned to the floor is the man she seems to be walking to.

Carmen cries in spite of himself as he watches Helen take the last walk as a single woman. His heart overflows knowing in a few moments she will soon be Mrs. Bontecou, his beloved wife. When she finally makes her way to him, the pastor addresses the congregations.

"Dearly beloveds, we are gathered here today to celebrate the joining of these two beautiful souls before you. Today they start the long and joyous journey of matrimony. The couple has prepared their own vows." He beams and looks to Carmen.

He looks at Helen for what seems to be an eternity in a glance. Her deep green eyes finally reflecting the peace he was feeling. It seems so long ago that they were about to die side by side. And now here they are, side by side, living in this rapturous moment. Helen quirks a smile at his pause and he remembers himself. Clearing his throat he takes her hand and thumbs it.

"Helen, you are my love, my life, for you I would conquer the world. I will open all of your doors, and stand guard to keep away the demons. Your soul I will hold, forever." —

Other Titles by Solange nicole:

My Beloved Tourniquet (Book 1 of the *Beloved Sereies)*
Chocolate Rose Will I Dream
HERE I STAND: In Love's Evil Embrace
On The Wings of Blue Rose
An Hour of Decadence
Book of Thoughts
SLAYERS (Featured short story *"Insatiable")*

 Follow her on Facebook, Tumblr, YouTube, and blog to get the latest on her books and the Beloved World.

Acknowledgements

Again, I would like to thank the city of New York for being awesome! The New York Ballet and the wonderful private school Avenues. Also a lovely thank you to Kaffe and the Touraine and Le Bernardin for being the backdrop to Helen and Carmen's romance.

And I would like to thank my fellow authors and editors for coming together and helping me make this book a possibility. And a big "I love you" to my two partners who helped with the long nights and the babysititing!

Here's to bigger and brighter things.

Avec amour,
S.

Check out the gripping tale of a haunted slayer, Sir John Badby, as he journeys to avenge his wife's sinful murder. Let yourself enjoy the titillating ride that is the life of a slayer. SLAYERS is an anthology of works by incredible authors bringing stunning originality and delightful horror. Twisted Core presents another winning 7DS title!

Solange nicole

Imagine a world…

www.ingramcontent.com/pod-product-compliance
Lightning Source LLC
Chambersburg PA
CBHW020738130626
46554CB00006B/2048